The Greek Constellations - Pisces

Stephan De Jonghe

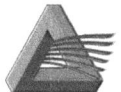

The Greek Constellations - Pisces

Copyright

For permission requests, write to the publisher at: stephansfolliclefarm@gmail.com

Ordering Information:

Special discounts are available on quantity purchases by book resellers, corporations, associations, and others. For details, contact the publisher at the email address above.

The Greek Constellations – Pisces, Second Edition 2026 by Stephan De Jonghe

ISBN 978-0-6453718-4-0 (paperback)

ISBN 978-0-6453718-5-7 (e-book)

Publisher: Stephan De Jonghe Publishing,

Hillarys, Perth, Western Australia, Australia 6025

Printer and distributor: Ingram Content Group, 1 Ingram Blvd. La Vergne, Tennessee USA 37086

In the footsteps of Homer and Hesiod.

From Astronomy to Mythology

How the constellations came to be named by the Greek God's.

Stephan J De Jonghe

Book One

The constellation

Pisces

The dedication

The dedication.

To say that my darling wife is the love of my life
is an understatement.

Deb is my best friend, soul mate, confidant, and life partner.

Among so many other things, we also share a love of books, and we have
a massive library on display in our home of books that we want to read.

Our topics include action, comedy, romance, science fiction, crime,
thrillers, and adventure.
We also have an impressive non-fiction collection.

My endeavours as an author represent a passion that
burns powerfully for me. I am driven to write.

I have many stories to tell and writing them and publishing them is my
way of contributing to other people's library's.

Writing involves many hours of research and then sitting in solitude,
slowly assembling the words that details a journey into a readable story.
One that was only previously an idea.

This takes a lot of patience and persistence.
After the story is put down, the process of editing begins.

Few non-writers understand that this stage can take as much five times longer than it takes to write the actual first draft.

My Deb gives me the support that I need to execute my writing passion. She not only supports my writing, but also enjoys reading the stories.

Her assistance with proof reading, feed-back on content, and editing, is invaluable.
Especially after I have become blind to my own errors.
She understands how important it is to me and to you, the reader, to get it right.

I dedicate these books to my wife as my thanks to her for her ongoing support, and for her contributions to the finished publications.

We are a team.

We both hope that you enjoy this series of books, and we look forward to your feedback.

Stephan and Deb De Jonghe

Special thanks

My special thanks go to Janey Emery – Renowned Australian artist, for giving me permission to use her art for the covers for my Greek Constellation series of books.

"I hope you enjoy her art and the story within these pages."
Stephan De Jonghe - Author

Janey's Story - Born in Narrogin, Western Australia, Janey Emery's interest in art began as early as 2 years of age and led to art becoming the central element in Janey's Childhood. Excelling in art throughout her school years Janey devoted herself to the art course provided by Balcatta Senior High school, where her passion for art only intensified.

Janey has been painting fulltime since 1991 and has attained a high degree of respect in the art world from peers and art lovers alike. Janey has won numerous distinguished artistic awards for her work and has sold many paintings throughout Australia and overseas. Janey Emery is achieving the recognition her distinctive artistic talents deserve.

Janey is Self-Taught in All Mediums with the exception of leisure courses undertaken in oil and water colours.

"Art has always played a part of who I am. From early childhood to now there has been a need for me to express myself through drawing and painting. I find peace in my craft, and I hope I bring that to my paintings."

"To me, my Art is like breathing. Painting is my life."
Janey Emery - Artist
https://www.janeyemery.art/

Authors note

This story is based on Greek mythology. The word Pisces however, is Latin for fishes. Many thousands of years ago, the origin of the constellation Pisces was one of the stories imagined by travellers and sailors.

Many of these stories owe some of their earlier history to the Phoenicians, Babylonians, and Mycenaean's, and were initially used to help ancient travellers remember star patterns as a nighttime navigational tool. Over time, these fascinating stories were greatly embellished on how the constellations came to be formed. The ancient Greeks called these constellations the "Katasterismoi" meaning, "the placing of the stars." They gave names and told stories about forty-eight out of the eighty-eight constellations that are recognised by the International Astronomical Union.

These mythologies were embellished as they were dauntlessly re-told with tales of gods encountering wild creatures, fighting fierce battles, and of course having lots of sex. After all, these men were away from home for lengthy periods of time. They shared these stories to entertain urban dwellers that they encountered, and from there the stories became legends, and for many people they became their religion.

A Greek poet and storyteller named Homer, was the first person to document these stories and he is most famous for the "Iliad" and the "Odyssey" which he composed some 2,800 years ago. Whilst very little is known about Homer, he is regarded by many as the founder of modern literature. His two main works were the first literary works to be taught formally to students.

Interestingly, there are over thirty-three film adaptations of the Odyssey, proving his works are still relevant to modern audiences.

Later, a poet named Hesiod, significantly contributed to Greek mythology and followed on from Homer's work. Together they are attributed with establishing ancient Greek religious customs, formal astronomy, the development of structured learning, documenting events, early economics, commercial farming, and time keeping.

The word "zodiac" originated from the Greek words "Zodiakos kuklos," meaning "circle of little animals". It wasn't until 50BCE that the first classical zodiac depicting the twelve astrological star signs in their current order was first depicted. It is known as the "Dendera zodiac."

During the 2nd century CE, a Greco-Roman astrologer and astronomer named Claudius Ptolemy worked on his documented Tetrabiblos into what is regarded as western astrology's primary source document and remains largely in use today. Also of note is that astronomers have named a crater on the Luna surface, and another on the surface of the planet Mars Ptolemaeus, in honour of Ptolemy and his contribution to astronomy.

The connection between Greek names and Roman names for the same deities came from their translation from one language to the other. In ancient Greek, Zeus is pronounced Dias. In Latin that became Djous Pater (Sky father) or Luppiter. In English this became Jupiter. Many names evolved in this way.

As an author, my goal is to turn what is known of the mythology, into an enjoyable story for today's reader.

Stephan J De Jonghe

My research dilemma

My research dilemma – another note from Stephan De Jonghe,

My "from astronomy to mythology" series of books posed some difficulties in terms of writing the stories into a logical chronology. Until the Iliad, and the Odyssey, no one had ever written any of the tales of titan's forming the world, or their ultimate defeat by the gods who eventually resided in Mount Olympus. These stories were imagined piecemeal, embellished, refined, and retold over a thousand-year period. Unlike history, which did happen on a linear timeline and can be plotted, the timeline that was used in these fictional stories was not relevant, and by their very nature, they were at the whim of the storyteller. Over the millennia, re-tellers of the stories frequently added details, and characters that were often inconsistent with the older stories. No one knew and essentially no one cared, as they were mostly just for entertainment.

For their more serious devotees, these stories were the basis for a religion, and many aspects of the stories were used to focus worshippers' attention. They were therefore treated by most people at the time as historical facts. They focused their attention on those gods and goddesses that were consistent with their beliefs and values. It is also important to remind the reader that for many thousands of years that storytelling was their main form of entertainment.

The best example that I can use to demonstrate the challenge of chronology, is referencing a main character known as Pandora. As she is known in Greek Mythology as the first human woman, and she gets featured by me in her own story. In mythology she was commissioned by Zeus and crafted by his son Hephaestus. This all happened when Zeus and Hera were already married. But in mythology Zeus had met and fallen in love with Europa, a human woman, who was alive before he married Hera, and before they he and Hera had a son for Zeus ask to make the first woman. This made it very challenging!

After many years of research, and many hours of pondering, I have finally found a workable theory that may explain this leap in the chronology (other than time travel). It stems from the term "first lady" as it applied to the wife of a male president of the United States. That woman isn't the first female to behave as a lady, nor is she the first woman in the USA. The term "first lady" is an idiom used to describe her role and her status within the US presidency. This term has caught on and is now use in many other countries. I therefore support the notion that Pandora as the "First Woman" as described in Greek Mythology was not the actual first woman created, but that she was created specifically to be the prime woman and the role model for all other women.

Whilst I feel fantastic about reaching this conclusion, I will now rewrite the Pandora story and include this realisation in my saga. For the devotees of my work. The first edition of the Pandora story treats Pandora as the first woman in creation (Such as Eve in the Adam and Eve story). This second edition treats Pandora as the prime human woman, and her creation was intended to become the role model for all human women.

Chronology

Chronology – Yet another note from Stephan De Jonghe,

As an author with a particular attention to detail, (at least I believe I do), the chronology of Greek mythological events became increasing important to me as the list of books planned for this series grew to thirteen.

I have therefore prepared a simple chronology (that may or may not be consistent with other writers of this genre) to assist readers in sorting out the sequence of events that occur in the stories that I am sharing with you (Spoiler alert!) and are the subject of ongoing revisions.

I believe that Greek Mythology Chronology should be a legitimised field of study all on its own. (Perhaps it already is?)

The Book.	The details of the event.
Pisces	Gaia forms the earth, oceans, and skies. She is the earth mother.
Pisces	Gaia gives birth to Uranus.
Pisces	Cronus is born and defeats Uranus when released from confinement.
Pisces	Aphrodite is born
Capricorn	Pricus is the father of the sea-goats.
Pisces	Cronus is crowned king of the Titans. Cronus marries his sister, Rea. Zeus is one of their six children.
Centaurus	Cronus mates with Philyra. Chiron is born.

Pandora	Prometheus creates a race of human men - The golden age
Pandora	Prometheus creates a second race of human men - The silver age
Pandora	Prometheus creates a third race of human men - The bronze age
Pisces	Zeus defeats Cronus and Zeus is crowned King of the Gods.
Pisces	Zeus marries Metis, Athena is born, but Metis dies.
Pisces	Zeus marries but then quickly divorces Themis.
Pandora	Prometheus creates a fourth race of human men - The iron age
Sagittarius	Crotus invents the bow and arrow.
Pisces	Zeus marries Hera. Ares, Eileithyia, Hephaestus, and Hebe are born.
Pisces	Aphrodite arrives at Mount Olympus and marries Hephaestus.
Pandora	Hephaestus creates Pandora as the first human woman.
Taurus	Zeus meets Europa.
Scorpio	Zeus mates with Leto. Apollo and Artemis are born.
Scorpio	Poseidon mates with Euryale. Orion is born.
Scorpio	Atalanta is recused as an infant and now runs with Artemis.
Aries	Zeus creates a cloud nymph and names her Nephele.
Aries	Poseidon mates with Theophane. Chrysomallos is born.
Aries	Nephele marries Athamas. The twins, Helle and Phrixus are born.
Aries	Chrysomallos rescues Helle and Prixus.

Ophiuchus	Apollo mates with Coronis. Asclepius is born.
Cancer/Leo	Zeus mates with Alkmene. Herakles is born.
Gemini	Zeus mates with Leda. Polydeuces and Castor are born.
Pisces	Aphrodite mates with Ares. Eros is born.
Scorpio	Orion meets and befriends Hephaistos.
Virgo/Libra	Zeus visits Themis and Astraea.
Cancer/Leo	Herakles is assigned the first of his ten labours.
Cancer/Leo	Herakles befriends Chiron.
Centaurus	Chiron befriends Herakles.
Gemini	Castor and Polydeuces join the Argo crew.
Cancer/Leo	Herakles joins Argo crew.
Gemini	Atalanta asks to join Argo crew.
Scorpio	Orion meets Artemis.
Centaurus	Chiron commences formally as a teacher.
Gemini	Herakles is inadvertently separated from the Argo.
Cancer/Leo	Herakles resumes his labours.
Scorpio	Orion duels with the giant scorpion.
Gemini	Jason and Argo crew return with the Golden Fleece.
Gemini	Calydonian Boar Hunt.
Gemini	Atalanta joins the Calydonian Boar Hunt.
Cancer/Leo	Herakles accidentally wounds Chiron.
Centaurus	Chiron makes his plea to Zeus.
Pisces	The Greeks and the Trojans start a war that lasts ten years.
Aquarius	Zeus meets Ganymede.
Cancer/Leo	Herakles becomes immortal and marries Hebe.

Stephan De Jonghe

1

The story of Pisces.

To many, Gaia is our earth mother and therefore she was everything that was, and everything that is yet to come. She tamed our planets savage volcanic crust and made the Earth habitable for all life. She is the soil, the land, the mountains, volcanoes, and the valleys. She was the jungles, forests, and fields, and all the flowers. She was the deserts, the mud, and the rocky coastline. She was the oceans, seas, sandy beaches, wild rivers, and the lakes. She was the air and could wield the wind to manifest torrential rain and fierce storms.

The Romans called our planet Terra and they renamed Gaia into Terra Mater which means Earth Mother. Later, our planet was named Earth which evolved from an old English word "*eorðe*" pronounced erothe, which means ground or soil. Terra Mater would in modern mythology become to be known to most of us as "Mother Nature". Now, her followers look to her as a kindly, nurturing, sedate, and even a sympathetic deity, who symbolises fertility and regrowth. But, at the beginning of time, Gaia was not so benevolent.

***

It was believed that Gaia had an earthly disposition. She was the primordial goddess in Greek Mythology, and was regarded as the creator and embodiment of the very planet in which we all live. She was taken seriously by followers who understood her beauty and her wildness. They also forgave her for her uncaring elements. She alone handcrafted the earth into the lands that we mortals today take for granted. She had a massive responsibility and usually handled it all with calm. But when she became angry, her fury was often vented with an unusual combination of catastrophic events. When Gaia was displeased, she could vent savagery on all the lands with fierce thunderstorms, howling winds, floods, avalanches, mudslides, volcanic eruptions, and earthquakes.

But way back when, in those early periods of Earth's creation, Gaia was lonely. Even with all her work to keep her busy, she felt the loneliness and isolation of being a sole Titan for all the earth, and so one day, she devised a solution to ward off her unhappiness. As an all-powerful entity, she decided she would manifest a child within her womb. Gaia decided to have a son and hoped that he would give more meaning to her existence. She would raise him, and he would be her companion, and when needed, her champion.

The following day she gave birth to a strong, healthy, baby boy, and Gaia was ecstatic. She named her son, Uranus, and she granted him lordship over of all the skies so that he could always surround her with all his love. Within days, Uranus was walking. Within a week, he was talking fluently, laughing at her jokes, and playing happily with his mother. Young Uranus quickly grew tall and statuesque, and he was given dominion over the skies as his mother Gaia continued to rule the earth. Even though she was very happy, she could see that as her son matured, that he became sadder. He was moping about, and he shunned conversation with her. His playful affections dwindled, and this made Gaia sad once more.

Eventually, Uranus melancholy worsened, and it caused him to rain many tears onto his mother's earth. They fell heavily from the skies, wetting her soils, burdening her rivers, and they were for the first time ever adding vast quantities of salt into her oceans, changing them forever. Gaia could not bear to see him weep so sadly, and so she reached up to give him comfort. It was then that he revealed to his mother about his desire to satisfy his manly needs. He wanted a woman to share his life with, and more importantly, to give him the physical pleasures that his loins constantly longed for. Gaia was initially horrified. She had never imagined she would be sharing her son with another woman. She lamented the problem and later decided that as she was his earth mother, that she would also become his earthly lover. She discussed this with him, and Uranus readily agreed. His face beamed happiness in anticipation of a sexual union.

They copulated many times, and for a while, it seemed that Uranus's urges were sated. He was happy, and for a while there were calm clear skies. But soon after their mating Gaia discovered to her joy, that she was pregnant, and later she gave birth to her second child, another son, who she named, Oceanus. She at once granted him dominion of the oceans and seas. However, Uranus was furious. He did not want to father children with Gaia. He did not want to share her with others, and so he flew into a rage and left.

Gaia missed Uranus terribly. She had plenty to keep her busy with a growing Oceanus, but she really missed being with her darling son, Uranus. While Gaia was absent and busy creating some fields and forests, Uranus visited with his son Oceanus, and he did not like what he saw. The young Titan was handsome, athletic, and seemingly burdened with excessive charm and enthusiasm. And so, he cast his son into the volcanic bowels of Gaia, and he made him a prisoner of Tartarus, deep within the earth. Uranus made certain that he was so well hidden, that it would be a eternity before his mother would ever see her beautiful Oceanus again.

When Gaia returned to their home, she learned of her youngest son's mysterious disappearance. She gave comfort to Uranus who was weeping over Oceanus's absence, as he was distressed, fearing the worst about his fate. Her nearness calmed him, and he quickly became aroused, and she was so pleased that he was happy, and that he wanted her again, that she copulated with him once more. So later Coeus was born, and again Uranus became angry. Later, during Gaia's absence, Coeus seemingly disappeared. It was because Uranus had sent him to Tartarus also.

And so, the cycle of comforting, procreation, and banishment continued with the births of Crius, Hyperion, Lapetus, Theia, Rhea, Themis, Mnemosyne, Phoebe, Tethys, Cronus, Bronte, Steropes, Arges, Cottus, Briareus, and Gyges.

Tartarus now held so many Titans, that they grumbled and rumbled with each new sibling's arrival. This caused much discomfort to Gaia their mother, who anguished forlornly over their disappearances. The one day, through a recently open volcanic vent, the banished Titans were able to communicate with their mother and tell her about their predicament. She flew into a rage, and for many weeks she spouted volcanic discharge, spewing molten rocks, thick burning ash, and masses of dense black smoke, high into the skies to show her displeasure to Uranus. But, even with all her venting she was only able to assist one son, Cronus in escaping from Tartarus' prison. Gaia was overjoyed to be reunited with her youngest son and she hugged and kissed him adoringly. Cronus was now fully grown, strong, and he was more than ready to revenge himself for his and his sibling's confinement. He was also fully committed to the liberation of his brothers and sisters. Gaia became conflicted. She adored Uranus and loved him so much, but also feared his wrath. She agreed she could not allow her other children to remain imprisoned, so she contrived a plan with Cronus on how to release the others, and to prevent future incarcerations from ever happening again. She insisted that it would be achieved without killing her beloved, Uranus. Reluctantly, Cronus agreed.

Gaia was so pleased with the plan that she relaxed, and the earth became calm once more. Uranus, on seeing that his mother was happy, assumed that she had now accepted the disposition of her other children. He decided to return to her in the hope that they would be reconciled, and that they would consummate their love once again. As Uranus descended from the skies, Cronus stepped out of his hiding place, and using a golden sickle that Gaia had given him, he reached up and grabbed his father's testicles, severing them savagely, and then he hurled them into the ocean. Uranus howled with the shock of the attack, and he was in considerable pain. In his anguish, he dived into the ocean to retrieve his testicles, but they were lost in the white foam that now rapidly formed from his spilled seed. For the first time since all creation, white foam was produced from the ocean's waves as they pounded the beaches and rocks at the shoreline.

The ground stirred around them. From the droplets of Uranus' spilled blood emerged many giants, nymphs, and the Three Furies, who were named Alecto, Megaera and Tisiphone who became the Titans of punishment. They quickly grew and all fled to populate the earth.

When Uranus returned to Gaia's side, he was a broken man. He was repentant and he agreed to immediately release their children from Tartarus. Soon they were all there, gathered around Cronus. He was their champion and they cheered him for their rescue. They all in turn embraced their overjoyed mother.

Uranus knelt before Cronus clearly demonstrating his acquiescence. He publicly recognised him as being the stronger, and more superior male. Gaia was conflicted. She was overjoyed to be reunited with her other children, but still wept to see Uranus so downcast. It was Gaia's plan that Cronus should have only threatened to sever his father's testes, and he was only to do so if he refused to release their children. She felt that Cronus had gone too far but even she could not undo what was done.

Later, it was agreed by all the reunited siblings, that Cronus should become their leader and he was decreed "King of the Titan's". Uranus' final words to his son before he returned to the skies were these. 'Be wary of your own sons, as one day, they too will betray you.'

***

Many people believe that all life on Earth originated from the oceans. One of the more interesting creations born in the ocean was an unusual female child. She was created directly from her father's seed when Uranus' severed testicles were cast into the ocean by Cronus. This manifestation happened quickly. Soon the young infant was drifting away from the shore having been caught in the outgoing tide, moving quickly away from the other Titans. They were totally unaware of her creation. As she floated away haplessly, a passing pod of dolphins noticed her plight and they quickly provided her with an abandoned giant scallop shell to use as a vessel. The dolphins kept her company as she was floating away above the watery depths, but they soon became bored and left her to go find a meal. Next, a kindly titan named Zephyrus, who was the west-wind, decided she needed his help and so he pushed her across the sea and up on a sandy beach on an island named Cyprus.

The young child continued to grow, and she was now the size of a toddler. She was able to climb out of the shell and walk some unsteady paces towards the trees, when she was greeted by four stunningly beautiful and unusually skilled women. They are known as the Seasons, or the Horai. Their names were Thallo, the bringer of blossoms who we know as spring. Auxo, the increaser of plants and growth who we know as summer. Carpo, bringer of food from the harvest, who we know as autumn. And Chioné, the protector of plants in slumber, who we know as winter. The four women closely examined the younger female. The four women wore dresses made from spun silk. They were breezy and free flowing. Thallo preferred green shades for her clothing. Auxo liked peach and orange coloured fabric. Carpo preferred yellow or red and often combine the two to positive effect. Chione' however wore dark clothing fitting her generally gloomy disposition.

'Hello little girl,' Auxo said as she smiled at the infant kneeling down to be closer to her level.

The infant blinked in surprise of being spoken too, but she looked thoughtful and then cautiously returned the smile. She looked to each of the women in turn. Three were smiling at her and she sensed safety. But the fourth one was frowning at her, and she somehow immediately knew that with her, there was risk.

'She's gorgeous,' Thallo proclaimed.

'Adorable,' confirmed another.

'She is,' the others chorused their agreement.

'I wonder where she came from,' Chioné pondered as she began looking out to sea as if she could find evidence of a vessel.

'I wonder who her parents are,' Thallo expressed her concern, and then looked up and down the beach as if she might see a reason for her sudden appearance.

'I think we will need to protect her until someone comes to claim her,' Auxo suggested.

'I think we should return her to her scallop shell, and then push her away from our island,' Chioné said, and she sounded cold and bitter as she if was proposing the infant's demise. 'Leave her to her own devises.'

The others looked at her in dismay.

'Don't you agree, she could mean trouble for all of us?' Chioné cautioned.

'No!' chorused the others.

'Maybe her fate was to come here to our island, and to be raised and cared for by us,' Carpo suggested happily.

'I wonder why she's naked,' Thallo mused.

'I think keeping here her is a mistake. I have a dark foreboding of future problems,' Chioné cautioned. She was staring intently at the child and frowned. 'She's growing,'

'How can this pretty little girl cause us any trouble?' Auxo demanded. She and the other women looked disappointingly at Chioné.

The child suddenly giggled, and they all turned to stare at the girl. When she arrived moments earlier, she had the appearance of a two-year-old. Now she could have easily been a five-year-old. The infant had been watching her would be rescuers throughout their conversation about her. She did not think it unusual that she not only understood every word they said about her, but she could also interpret the consequences of what they were saying.

She walked toward Auxo and flung her arms out to her and almost leapt into her arms. Auxo reached down to catch the child and held her in a protective embrace. The child snuggled into Auxo, pushing her head into the nape of her neck. She then kissed Auxo and smiled generously at her.

'Aww,' Thallo and Carpo chorused.

'She must be cold,' Chioné reasoned.

'She doesn't feel cold,' Auxo responded embracing the child. Then she observed 'But, she is getting heavier,' she explained as she adjusted her hold on young girl.

'She'll be a nuisance,' Chioné cautioned.

Thallo naturally adopted a leadership role whenever there were grumblings between the four women. She announced her assessment to their current predicament. 'I believe we have a duty to protect and care for this child for as long as she is with us, or, until she is old enough to decide for herself. We three, Auxo, Carpo, and I, will provide for her and raise her.' She then turned to face Chioné. 'I believe you should keep your distance from her. I do not want our decision to divide us, as we are the Seasons and must remain cohesive and unified, but when it comes to the care of this child, we shall do this without you.'

Chioné stared coldly at Thallo. She then looked at the girl and then back at Thallo. 'That suits me just fine, so I will agree,' she conceded. She turned and walked away leaving the others to care for their new ward.

    ***

The girl continued to grow quickly, but for some reason she stubbornly refused to wear any clothing. The climate was idyllic, so she never felt the heat of summer, or the cool of winter, and she also felt free and uninhibited. She loved frolicking naked on the beach, or swimming in clear pools of fresh water, or being chased by her guardians through the lush vegetation, delighting in imaginary games with the three woman who adored playing with her. Her carers were mostly unconcerned, as there were no males on their island, only the five females.

She had a good appetite, and she ate a wide variety of foods with enthusiasm. Her language skills developed rapidly to a point where she amazed the three Seasons. She spoke clearly, articulately, and effortlessly, and just like any female child, she spoke continuously. She asked so many questions about their island home, and the nature of the abundant plants that fed and sheltered them. She desperately wanted to know all about their life experiences.

Soon her pubis sprouted hair that was so wispy and fine that it was almost transparent. Shortly after that, her breast buds appeared, and they swelled and grew into magnificently proportioned breasts. Her hands were soft and warm and were quickly given to administer gentle caresses and massages that the women welcomed. She grew long graceful legs which made her tall, and developed voluptuous curves for her calves, thighs, and buttocks. She had a strong flat stomach, and proud shoulders, with a long, graceful neck that supported her magnificently shaped head.

Her face was beautifully proportioned, and it was framed with long gossamer straw-coloured hair, which when caught in the sun's rays, radiated magnificently. Her hair also seemed to glow softly in the dark. Her complexion glowed with gentleness and passion, and her tanned skin was soft, smooth, and unblemished. Her eyes were vivid blue and looked sincere and kindly, and they twinkled with a hint of mischievousness and excitement. Her lips were full and moist. Her smile was captivating and genuine, and she quickly learned to use apt words to calm the darkest mood in her recipients. She also had a magnificent singing voice, and whenever she was alone, she would amuse herself with songs of her own creation. Despite the three Seasons' best attempts to clothe her, the young confident woman preferred to walk about naked, and she only wore the skimpiest of clothing when chided into them by Auxo, the favourite of her adopted mothers.

The girl also had an unquenchable hunger for knowledge. She wanted to know all about the plants and their amazing powers and properties. She learned about which plants were good for food, and which plants could do her harm. She learned which plants could give her powers over others, and she even tried them on the Seasons, much to their amusement. She also learned that some plant odours would make her more appealing to others, whereas other plant odours would do much to repel those who she deemed unwanted. Her favourite plants were roses and myrtle. She also loved being with the family of swans who followed her about with loving devotion, and the small flock of cooing doves that came to her for a daily feed of seeds that she prepared especially for them.

The Seasons often found her in the rose garden talking animatedly with the swans and doves who sang back to her with their seemingly knowing responses.

***

Thallo loved the young woman as if she were her own daughter and therefore, she especially wanted to teach her about the wonders of the four seasons. Thallo's speciality was spring as she had the powers and responsibility behind the re-emergence of flowers and leaves on all the plants that had slumbered during winter. She shared with her the knowledge of that power. The one that gave the burst of energy that transforms seemingly dead plants back into life once more. It was this knowledge that gave the women their eternal beauty and youthfulness. Thallo made her student promise to never share these secrets with mortals, and that she could only ever use them for herself. She readily agreed, and she and Thallo never told the other Seasons that she had learned her secrets. It was in this way that the woman was given full control over her own perpetual beauty.

Before long, the young girl had grown fully into an adult woman. She was not just beautiful, she was stunning. She was perfectly proportioned, and her skin was lustrous. Her smile was enchanting, and she used it cunningly to get her own way. But despite all of her beauty and her charms, the young woman still did not have any positive effect on Chioné.

Chioné was exceptionally skilled and knew how to prepare the plants to survive in the coldest climates. She alone had the knowledge of what to do to prepare the plants to shed their withering foliage in the Autumn. How knew how they survived being dormant in the winter, until the weather was warm enough for Thallo to reignite their growth with flowers and leaves in the Spring.

Mischievously, Chioné prepared a potion from a sweet-smelling nectar and poured it into a cup favoured by the young woman and placed it where she would find it. She added a gift basket containing a multitude of different coloured rose petals that made the gift look like it came from Thallo. The woman was delighted with the gifts, and so she eagerly consumed the liquid.

The potion Chioné had prepared was certainly powerful enough to kill the young woman, but as her fate would have it, she did not die. It could have been because the woman was born from the seed of a Titan and was therefore immortal. Or perhaps it was because her body was already fortified with the rejuvenating potions given to her by Thallo. Instead of killing her, the combination of these two potions, now intermingled in the blood stream of the woman's body, causing her to fall into a deep comatose sleep.

Despite the best efforts and loving devotions of the other three Seasons, they were unable to awaken her. The woman slept without ageing, and without deterioration, for a lengthy immeasurable age.

***

Cronus fully intended be a benevolent god. He aspired to rule the Titans with kindness and compassion. So, it was with regret that he returned the three Cyclopes - Bronte the god of thunder, Steropes the god of lightening, and Arges the god of light, along with the three, monstrous hundred handed brothers, the Hokatonchires, who were named Cottus, Briareus, and Gyges, to Tartarus. He felt he had to do so because they had openly and persistently defied him. The remaining Titans were pleased as his lament gave them hope of just rule, but his decisiveness inspired confidence.

Cronus decided he would be married to his favourite sister, Rhea. She accepted his proposal eagerly and together they had six children, three daughters they named Demeter, Hestia, and Hera, and three sons they named, Hades, Poseidon, and lastly, Zeus. Despite having a wonderful and loving relationship with Rhea, Cronus remained forever fearful of his father's dire warning that one day one of his children will challenge and defeat him.

Cronus solved this problem by swallowing each of their newborn babies' whole. In this way, he would prevent them from growing up, and to one day plot to overthrow him. Rhea pleaded for her children, but Cronus insisted that he knew what he was doing. However, when Zeus was born, Rhea rebelled, and she gave Cronus a rock that was shaped like a baby wrapped in a blanket, which he happily swallowed believing it to be the child. Zeus was later secretly sent to his cousin Metis, who cared for him and raised him to adulthood. Zeus's siblings not only survived their incarceration, but they also grew into adults whilst inside of Cronus. As they were immortal they could not be destroyed.

When Zeus had grown into a strong and handsome man, he returned home to his mother, Rhea. She was so very pleased to see her son, but she was immediately concerned for Cronus's reaction to learning of his son's escape from his internment. Together, they quickly formed a plan on how to release his brothers and sisters from Cronus's stomach. Rhea knew Cronus would not recognise her adult son as being his own, and so she hid him in full view as Cronus's new cupbearer. She arranged with Metis to supply her with a powerful drug, an emetic mixture which she combined with honeyed wine in a large cup for Zeus to serve to his father. The powerful emetic made him sick and forced Cronus to disgorge the contents of his stomach. First to come out was the stone that was supposed to have been baby Zeus. Then, one after the other, all five siblings came out.

They were grateful about being released, but they were also angry with their father for his treatment of them The six adult children decided to call themselves Gods and Goddesses to separate themselves from the Titans. They readily agreed to join forces to battle for power against Cronus and his followers. This evolved into a prolonged war that was called the Titanomachy. It pitted Zeus and his brothers and sisters in a unremitting battle against Cronus and the other Titans who remained loyal to their king.

As they were all immortal and had matching powers, the battle between Gods and Titans continued for an eternity. To turn the tide in the Gods favour, Zeus arranged for the confined Cyclopes and the monstrous Hokatonchires to be released from Tartarus, but only if they agreed to side with him against Cronus, which they readily did. The Cyclopes were superb craftsman and soon presented Zeus, Poseidon, and Hades, with powerful new weapons. They gave Zeus many lightning bolts and thunderclaps so that he could hurl them great distances into his enemy and destroy them. They gave Poseidon a magnificently forged trident that he could use to split the earth before his enemies and he loved it so much that he carried it everywhere. Lastly, they gave Hades a helmet of darkness that rendered him invisible.

Armed with their new weapons and with renewed resolve, Zeus hurled lightning bolts at Cronus and his followers. Vast forests were soon engulfed with flames and smoke filled the skies. His lightning boiled oceans, producing blinding steam, and when it combined with the tree smoke it confused the Titans. Hades, wearing his invisibility helmet, slipped into Cronus' stronghold and stole all of his weapons. Poseidon followed and attacked Cronus with his trident. They could not injure Cronus, but the two were able to distract Cronus long enough for Zeus to hurl his most powerful lightning bolt at their now defenceless father. Injured, Cronus quickly conceded defeat to his three sons.

The defeated Titans were judged and then sentenced to be confined to Tartarus. They were locked behind marble gates and a bronzed threshold. Despite their own release from their confinement, most of the monsters that Zeus had freed agreed to become the guards and watch over the imprisoned Titans. For them, it felt like a reward as justice was served.

***

For his efforts and natural leadership, it was mutually agreed by his siblings, that Zeus would be crowned their King and would be the ruler of the Gods. Between them they decided that Zeus should rule over the lands and the skies. Poseidon chose to rule the oceans and the seas And Hades willingly agreed that he would happily rule the underworld. The brother's formed an unbreakable bond agreeing to never challenge each other or interfere in each others domain.

Zeus next established a mountain community for all present and future gods and goddesses to live, work, and play. It was established near the top of the highest mountain in the known world. There, he set up a council of Gods, for he believed in a consultative approach to important decision making. The founding gods and goddesses included Demeter, who became the goddess of the harvest and agriculture, Hestia, who became the goddess of the hearth and domesticity, Hera, who became the goddess of women, marriage, marital harmony. They also included Prometheus, the God of foresight, who despite being a Titan, had cleverly decided to side with Zeus and the other gods during the battle as he could foresee their ultimate victory.

Hades agreed to venture from the underworld to attend their meetings, as did Poseidon from the sea. Zeus, as the king was their chairperson, and for most of the time their council was run as a democracy.

He named their home, Mount Olympus.

***

The seasons changed as the seasons do. The cycle of life continued unimpeded by the clashes of gods and titans. After learning the young woman's fate, Chioné continued to keep her distance from the three others. They did occasionally meet with Chioné to discuss the change from Autumn to Winter, and then again to plan for the return to Spring. Thallo, Carpo, and Auxo remained puzzled about the young woman's continuing eternal slumber. After discussing season's cycle, they once again raised their concerns with Chioné.

'Our beautiful daughter is now fully grown, but sadly she remains in a deep sleep,' Thallo explained to Chioné.

'I don't know anything about that,' Chioné snorted. She turned and hastily departed.

'How strange,' Carpo commented.

'Chioné is weird,' Auxo agreed.

'She never liked or trusted her,' Thallo observed.

'Chioné intensely dislikes our beloved daughter,' Auxo added.

Carpo stirred and then spoke. 'You know, I am wondering if it is a coincidence that as she is responsible for plants to make them slumber if she has anything to do with keeping our daughter perpetually asleep.

'What did you say?' Thallo was incredulous.

'Well, Chioné arranges for plants to go dormant, and now our girl sleeps much like plants do in winter,' Carpo smiled, pleased with her own observation. 'It is like she is in hibernation.'

'So, we should be able to revive her somehow. As if it became spring.'

'Do you think Chioné is responsible?' Auxo queried, now hopeful that they may be on the path to solving the mystery.

'Sadly, I now think that Chioné gave her a potion intending to kill her, but as I had given her the potion to give her everlasting youth and beauty, Chioné's potion only succeeded in putting her into slumbering sleep.'

'So, what can we do?' Auxo asked.

'Carpo, you have the powers that turn flowers into fruit,' Thallo asked rhetorically as she already knew the answer. It was soon obvious to the others that she was now forming a workable plan.

'Yes, of course,' Carpo agreed and smiled.

'If you prepare your potion, we'll give it to her. I think that might be just enough to revive her,' Thallo suggested hopefully.

The others enthusiastically agreed, and so Carpo expertly prepared her potion. Soon they were by the young woman's side. They supported her body upright and they were carefully administering some of the special fruiting potion into the young woman's mouth. As the drops hit the woman's tongue, their power instantly started to take effect. Soon she was opening her mouth searching for more of the nectar. They continued to slowly feed her more of the potion and then slowly her eyes opened. They gently dispensed the rest of the cup's contents into the woman's mouth, which the woman eagerly drank and she quickly she became fully conscious. She stretched away her slumber, totally unaware that she had been asleep for such a long time.

'I'm hungry,' she declared and then grinned expectantly at her loving and benevolent mother's.

The three women laughed and then sighed in relief.

'Why don't you go and prepare us all some food,' Thallo suggested.

The woman smiled happily and then leapt out of the bed to do as she was bid.

As the young woman gathered the food for the four of them to eat, the three Seasons discussed what had just happened in whispered tones.

'She seems none the wiser for her slumber.'

'And she hasn't aged at all,' agreed another.

'We must punish Chioné for what she has done,' Auxo demanded.

'No. She is our equal, so we dare not. Besides, we need her as much as she needs us,' Carpo countered.

'I agree that we cannot punish her, despite the concern she imposed on us for our sweet girl's wellbeing,' Thallo conceded. 'But we must now agree to pretend that her slumber never happened. She would not be pleased to learn of Chioné's plot against her, and so as nothing good will come from her knowing. We should keep it as our secret.

The others nodded their agreement.

Thallo continued. 'But I also believe that the time has come for her leave us. We must make her safe from her from any future attacks by Chioné.'

'Where will we send her?' Auxo was concerned.

'I think she should go to live with Zeus and the other Gods at Mount Olympus to . Clearly, she belongs with them, and so I believe she'll have a better life among her equals.'

It was agreed that Thallo would make the preparations for the woman to leave them, and that she should continue her life's journey among the Gods and Goddesses at Mount Olympus.

The three Seasons were unaware that Chioné was hiding in the bushes eavesdropping in on their plans. She smiled in relief after learning about the young woman's imminent departure.

Later that evening, the four women were talking happily after clearing the remnants of their meal.   Then suddenly the young woman queried, 'When will we see Chioné again?'

'Soon. She mostly rests during our active months,' Thallo replied.

'She can be a bit lacking in warmth or affection,' Carpo added.

'She does her role well, protecting plants during the coldest part of the year so that they can flourish once more in the springtime,' Thallo defended.

'Why haven't you ever given me a name?' the woman asked. She did not sound angry, she just sounded curious.

The three Seasons looked at her with surprise.

'We knew a time would come when you would want a name of your own, 'Auxo said kindly with a smile. 'We thought you would choose your own name when you were ready,'

'So, how would you like to be known?' Carpo asked.

'I don't know,' the woman replied. She frowned uncharacteristically and looked puzzled.

The four later settled themselves to sleep, and for the first time since the pretty little girl arrived at their shores, they heard her crying. As she sobbed, they knew that her misery came from her lack of identity. Each of the three Seasons resolved to help her find a name, and they would start encouraging her to find her purpose. The following morning when the three Seasons awoke, the woman was gone.

They later found her on the beach where she had arrived onto their island, she looked enormous sitting awkwardly inside her long-abandoned scallop shell, and she appeared to be talking to the wind. As they approached her, they heard her speaking, 'So, your name is Zephyrus, and you pushed me in this little shell, to this island, across the sea from where I was born?' The woman asked seeking clarification from the wind.

'Yes,' the breeze whispered back.

'Who are my parents and where are they now?' she demanded.

'You have none,' Zephyrus replied.

'So how was I born?' The woman was querulous.

'You emerged from the sea foam, the Aphros,' Zephyrus explained as he blew away, leaving them to ponder this revelation.

The young woman sat in stunned silence. She had just learned about some of her history and was now trying to process it.

The three Seasons took turns to embrace her and to give her comfort. But she suddenly she cried out in excitement. 'I have a name!'

'What is it?' Auxo demanded, 'How would you like to be called?'

'I am Aphros!' She declared proudly.

'You can't be called, "sea foam",' Thallo disagreed pulling a face in disgust.

'How about we call you Aphro….di…te?' Carpo suggested.

'Aphrodite.' The woman thought it over. 'I like it,' she declared. 'In fact, I love it. From now on you should call me, Aphrodite.'

'They laughed and hugged, and all were pleased with the name.

The most beautiful woman in all the lands, for now and for all time, now had a name. she would be known forever as Aphrodite. Now, they must help her find her purpose so that she can add meaning to her life.

That night Thallo, Carpo, Auxo, and Aphrodite, talked long into the night. They collectively agreed that the time was right for Aphrodite to leave their island. They also agreed that due to the nature of her birth, and her rapid growth, meant that she was a either a Titan or a Goddess. They agreed that they should send her to Mount Olympus to meet with the other Gods and there she would discover what her future would be when living with them. Aphrodite was excited at the prospect of meeting others like her, but she was also sad to be leaving her adopted mothers, and so she promised sincerely to visit often.

Before they had settled themselves to rest, Chioné entered their shared bed chamber. They all knew that she would soon assert herself as the time of winter was quickly approaching.

'Chioné, I am now ready to leave your home,' Aphrodite explained to Chioné before she could speak. Aphrodite smiled, but as always, her smile failed to win over this woman.

'I know,' Chioné replied coldly. 'I too have been busy. I have arranged for Zeus to come here to our island to collect you. He will arrive soon after dawn, and you will leave with him to join the other gods at Mount Olympus.'

The three other women felt their tears forming, but they remained silent.

***

Zeus enjoyed flying and his preferred form was that of a giant eagle. He was respected and feared by the other birds and that suited him. He could fly swiftly, and gracefully, and that suited him also. He could see better with his eagle eyes than he could with his own eyes, and he really appreciated that advantage. He practiced the eagle's techniques of riding thermals to gain height and flying with wind currents behind him to gain speed, and to press his wings to his sides for rapid descents. His claws were razor sharp, but short enough so when retracted he could transport the most fragile people with grace and without inflicting any injury. Yes, shooting the breeze as a magnificent and respected eagle, suited him very much.

His journey from Mount Olympus to Cyprus was uneventful, and Zeus landed gracefully onto the beach and casually transformed back into his human form. His clothing reformed with him, so he never appeared dressed in any way other than how he expected to be. He looked about him unsure of who or what would greet him. The idea that sprung into his mind that inspired him to fly to Cyprus was a little confusing to him, but the compulsion he felt for doing so continued to remain high. At the very least he would have the opportunity to consult with the four Seasons who he had adopted as his daughters. He would learn from them the details of seasonal forecasts that he and his fellow Olympians would need to be aware of regarding the agricultural needs of the mortals under their protection. He was not sorry that he had made the journey but he was curious to learn more about why it felt so important to do so.

Chioné stepped out of the vegetation and onto the sandy pathway and calmly walked toward Zeus. He recognised her at once.

'Hello Chioné,' Zeus spoke in familiar terms with all the Seasons.

'Father,' Chioné acknowledged. 'We've been expecting you,' she informed him.

Hugging was not Chioné 's thing. She could be cold and unemotional by Zeus's reckoning. He said nothing, but he gave her the look that encouraged Chioné to elaborate. 'Zephyrus told me,' she replied.

'The answer was blowing in the wind,' Zeus confirmed nodding his understanding, aware that his attempts at frivolity were often lost on her.

'Do you want to know why you are here?'

'Yes.'

'An interloper lives among us. We don't know where she came from, but we are confident that she is either a Titan or of Olympian ancestry.'

'So, your guest is a female,' Zeus was curious.

'She is,' Chioné confirmed. 'We would like you to take her with you to Mount Olympus. She does not belong here, and she has disturbed our routine and taken advantage of our hospitality for too long.' She paused, but then added. 'I fear if she remains here that there will be many fierce storms this winter.'

Zeus studied her but said nothing.

So, she continued. 'This will result in damaged crops which would be disastrous.'

'I suppose it would be better for everyone if I take her to Mount Olympus with me,' Zeus offered. 'That might help keep things calm.' he paused and then added, 'I am looking forward to meeting your unwanted guest. Where will I find her?'

'She is with Thallo, Carpo, and Auxo. They have been mothering her. You will find them in the summer clearing,' Chioné explained as she pointed toward the path and gestured to Zeus that he should follow it to find them.

'I see,' Zeus replied and nodded that he understood. She can be unpleasant at times, but he simply shrugged and headed toward the path.

As he rounded a corner has saw three of the Seasons talking with the most beautiful woman that he had ever seen in his entire existence. She stood before him tall, proud, and confident, and as a bonus, she was naked. He stood and stared at her in lustrous fascination. He soon felt a stirring within his loins, and he made no attempt to quell his desire to hold this woman against him, and now desired to be joined with her in a lengthy, mutually satisfying, coupling.

'Zeus!' A woman's voice interrupted his thoughts, and his impending swelling rapidly subsided.

He broke off his gaze and sought out the voice that had just called out to him. 'Thallo,' Zeus acknowledged lifting his eyebrows in mock surprise that she was here.

Thallo, Carpo, and Auxo, marched intently toward Zeus. He took a defensive step backwards and the three women broke out into smiles and chuckled. They were clearly happy to see him.

'Don't worry, we won't hurt you,' Carpo laughed.

'Not unless you plan to seduce or hurt Aphrodite, that is,' Auxo clarified.

'Is that her name?' Zeus looked at the beautiful woman again, unaffected by the Season's assertions. He was already thinking about mutual pleasuring.

Aphrodite was also curious. It was the first time she had ever seen a male, and she had quickly decided that she wanted to learn all about him.

'Aphrodite,' Auxo spoke for the three women. 'This is Zeus,' she introduced. 'He is the king of all the God's, and he lives at Mount Olympus.'

Auxo stepped closer to Zeus and explained in a discrete whisper. 'Father, we think Chioné may have plans to do some harm to Aphrodite. You must take her with you for her protection.'

'She'll be safe with me, I will protect her,' he whispered in reply and grinned boyishly.

'I am ready to leave this place and go with you to Mount Olympus,' Aphrodite spoke to Zeus in a familiar tone.

'There's no hurry,' Zeus told the group. He studied Aphrodite intently, his eyes widening. 'We should get to know each other a little better before we leave.'

'Father!' Thallo cautioned.

Zeus sighed. 'It would be prudent for me to explain to Aphrodite the nature of her future life at Mount Olympus. I need to prepare her before I present her to the Gods and Goddesses that live there. Without some insight, she might be a little overwhelmed by our antics,' he defended.

'We have already instructed Aphrodite about what to expect about her life at Mount Olympus,' Carpo explained. 'We believe she is prepared.'

'I'm sorry but I will need to test your premise for myself,' Zeus concluded. He turned to Aphrodite. 'Besides, do you need to pack?'

'I am wearing everything I own,' Aphrodite smiled mischievously. She totally understood the affect that her nakedness was having on him and she was enjoying it.

'You are definitely my kind of woman,' Zeus concluded with a nod and a grin.

Before the three Seasons could object, Zeus whisked himself and Aphrodite to the other side of the island. They were well away from any interference or meddling that Thallo, Carpo, or Auxo could conjure.

'Wow,' Aphrodite was impressed.

'Gods have many powers,' Zeus explained. 'And, I have more than most,' he added with a smile.

'And I hear that you are their king,' Aphrodite complimented him.

'Yes,' Zeus agreed. 'And you are the most beautiful woman that I have ever met.'

'Are you qualified to judge beauty?' Aphrodite asked with a smile and a twinkle of teasing from her eyes.

Zeus laughed. 'I most certainly am.' He leaned forward and kissed her fully on the lips. Aphrodite willingly reciprocated and further responded by pressing her body firmly up against his.

The affect was immediate, and Zeus quickly disrobed, and he wrapped his long arms about her in a lover's urgent embrace. But then suddenly, he stopped and pushed her away from him.

'What's wrong?'

'Nothing... I just...'

'Am I too much for you?' Aphrodite asked, clearly bemused by his awkwardness.

No, um yes, I think it is too soon.' Zeus said as he stumbled out his reply. He felt concerned and decided he needed time to ponder the situation.

'Too soon. Why?' she looked about the area and could see no-one. 'Our timing could not be more perfect.' She reached up placing her arms over his shoulders drawing him toward her.

He ducked from under them and stepped back. 'Let me explain.'

She stood before him, legs parted, her nipples erect, and she had her hands on her hips. She forced a smile as she waited patiently for the king of the Gods to gather his thoughts. Zeus sat down and he rested his back on the trunk of a tree. He shook his head in disbelief. 'I cannot believe that I am saying this, but I think we should not be doing it.'

'Doing what? So far you haven't done anything.'

'Sex, copulating, joining groins...' Zeus spelled it out.

'I would really like to give it a try... I have seen animals doing it and they seem happy enough,' Aphrodite concluded.

'Sex is... well, it can be complicated,' Zeus retorted.

'It seems straight forward to me.' Aphrodite was not yet convinced that there was a problem. 'You make your thingy hard again and you put it inside me, here.' She pointed unabashedly toward her groin.

'You still are a virgin, aren't you?' Zeus queried.

'I do not know what that is,' Aphrodite admitted.

'You've never had sex,' Zeus explained.

'No. But it looks like it should be easy enough to do, and I have been led to understand that it can be extremely pleasurable for both persons.'

'It can be... and it should be...' Zeus agreed. 'But that is not always the result.'

'Do you lack the necessary experience and skills...?' she challenged.

'No! Of course not. I am... exceptionally skilled.' Zeus was aghast at her assertion. He then relaxed and smiled at her. 'You are a virgin. There are things to consider when you are with a virgin.'

'Like what?' She questioned him now feeling frustrated with their lack of activity. Her earlier excitement, and the anticipation of experiencing sex with him was now fading fast, and she was beginning to feel let down.

'You know.' Zeus looked at Aphrodite hopefully but then realising that clearly she did not. Her posture was unchanged, and the smile never left her face. It was almost like she was inviting him, or even daring him to copulate with her. He sighed heavily.

She then capitulated graciously. 'We do not have to do it if you are not up for it. I promise you that I won't tell anyone that you could not get your thingy hard enough to put it inside of me.'

Zeus was staggered at what she had just accused. 'No.' he said sounding fraught and looked down at his flaccid member and then back up to her face. 'It is not that I can't do it. It is more that I believe that we should not do it,' he concluded.

'I think we should.' Aphrodite moved several steps toward him and again stood with her legs wide apart, invitingly. Do you not desire me?' She mocked incredulity rocking her hips toward him.

'Oh, yes I do. I really do desire you. I think you are the most desirable woman I have ever met. I think the whole world will see you as desirable woman, and that is going to be a big part of my problem,' Zeus tried to explain.

'Do you think that I am I too desirable?' Aphrodite was confused.

'Yes,' Zeus agreed.

Aphrodite said nothing. Her smile faded from her face, and she looked imploringly at Zeus for additional explanation.

Zeus sighed heavily once more. 'You need to understand that I am married to Hera. She has been on and on at me about all the women I have been having sex with. It is really not my fault that my sexual needs and urges are greater than hers. I am actually doing her a favour by spreading my sexual liaisons about with other women, and not pestering her about it all the time, like I did when we were first married. Unfortunately, she does not see it the same way as I do, and she wants me to slow down and settle into a nice safe routine and be just with her. So, as it happens, just before I came here to meet you, we had had our deep and meaningful discussion. For some unknown reason, I found myself promisingly her that I would not have sex with anyone else but her. Or at least until we could work out a mutually agreeable solution to satisfy both our sexual needs.' He then drew a deep breath. 'I am sorry Aphrodite, but my wife has an uncanny habit of knowing every time that I have done it with someone else. Normally, that doesn't bother me at all, but this time, for some reason it does. It could be because I have only just made that promise to her, that now it feels too weird to break it. Do not concern yourself. I know that you will get plenty of invitations for great sex from the other gods at Mount Olympus. They will all want you. I want you! But...' he shook his head in disbelief. 'But I cannot have you. Besides the Seasons will know and they do not want us to do it either, and I do not want to upset them, or make them angry, because that would disappoint a lot of people and their crops might fail all because we did it.

'So, you are still going to take me to Mount Olympus, and you believe that I will eventually have great sex with a different God when we get there?' Aphrodite clearly was not impressed with Zeus's lame attempt at claiming his fidelity. She wanted to have sex now. She realised that she had been waiting a long time for this opportunity. She felt ready.

'I can guarantee it.' Zeus hoped she was beginning to understand and that she was accepting his explanation.

'But you said you were the best. Will the others be as good as you are, at doing it?' Aphrodite sounded disappointed.

Zeus shook his head. 'No, they won't be. It is true that I am the best....' Zeus tried to make himself seem almost modest.

'You are now asking me to accept less than best when you stated that I was the most beautiful and desirable woman you had ever met?' Aphrodite did not look happy with Zeus's rejection.

Zeus said nothing. He stood up and wiped the sand off his skin.

'I am ready to leave,' she told him.

He nodded. 'We should say goodbye to your mothers before we go.'

'Thank you.'

'They should have some suitable clothing for you to wear. It can get cold when we are flying, and you will feel more presentable wearing clothing when we arrive at Mount Olympus. The Goddesses tend to be excessively judgmental.'

She looked at herself and smiled. From now on she would have to consider other people's opinions of her. It would take some getting used to.

Zeus transformed once more into the giant eagle. He turned his back to her and motioned for her to climb on his back and she did so. He gracefully jumped into the air and then with powerful beats of his wings, he flew them both back to her three worried mothers.

Zeus landed and Aphrodite shook her head as she dismounted. Her three mothers each smiled their understanding. They all felt relief that nothing sexual between them had happened.

Thallo then revealed a long flowing white gown that was woven with the finest silk. It looked magnificent and Aphrodite beamed with joy as she slipped over her head and down over her body. She smoothed the silk dress with her hands and for the first time she felt fabulous wearing clothing. They then decorated her hair with sunflowers.

Zeus nodded his appreciation of the way she looked. Even clothed she was still stunningly beautiful.

Aphrodite next hugged each of her beloved mothers in a tearful farewell.

Zeus morphed and Aphrodite climbed on his back once more. With several strong beats of his wings, he lifted the two of them from the ground and flew them toward Mount Olympus.

Aphrodite's adopted mothers watched the departing eagle with mixed emotions.

Chioné left the cover of the trees and stood beside them. She spoke calmly has she announced, 'Many ships have arrived on the far side of our island. They are brimming with families and livestock. Our home is suddenly being populated with humans.

***

Gaia learned of Aphrodite's existence from Zephyrus. As he was passing by her, she had nonchalantly asked him if he had any interesting news. His reply shocked her. He calmly and casually whispered that he knew of a beautiful woman name who was recently named Aphrodite, and that she had been born from the foam that had formed from Uranus' spilled seed. He also explained that she had been raised and educated by the four Seasons on Cyprus. Next, he told her that she would soon leave Cyprus to be with Zeus and live at Mount Olympus. Before she could ask Zephyrus for more details, the west wind had already moved on.

Gaia was confused but she knew that she felt deeply troubled by this news. As she pondered, everything everywhere became still. The wind speeds dropped, the ocean waves settled, and the rivers slowed. Waterfalls trickled. Birds and insects landed and became still. Animals laid down to rest. She thought mostly about the fact that a daughter created from Uranus' spilled seed, would soon be in league with the enemy of her beloved children. She could become a risk to Titans everywhere. Any of Zeus's offspring would definitely bring about more trouble for her own. Then suddenly she became furious. The oceans and skies became stormy. Birds and insects took flight. Animals everywhere growled and barked and yapped at nothing. Rivers and streams rose, and waterfalls gushed. Gaia then decided to unleash a monster at the island home of the four Seasons, with specific orders to kill Aphrodite before she met Zeus and conspired against all Titans.

Gaia aggressively slapped the ground, and she was instantly pregnant. Her belly quickly swelled, and she soon gave birth to a hideous male monster. He had hundreds of venomous snake heads, alternating with fire breathing dragon heads that grew out from his neck, shoulders, and torso. He roared and hurled scorching fire with his dragon mouths and spat out deadly venom from his snake fangs. He did this with astonishing accuracy. He also had over a hundred muscular arms each with massive hands that he formed into deadly fists. He launched fire bolts from his eyes. He had massive wings that grew from his back when needed and they could easily support his bulk and with them he could fly very fast and great distances. From his mouths, he could also muster up fierce, destructive, and unrelenting winds. His size and strength surpassed all other monsters that had ever resided on Earth. Gaia was proud of her creation, and she named him Typhon.

Typhon could transform himself into human form. When he did so, he became a very unpleasant looking man. He also reeked of obnoxious body odour and had offensive foul-smelling breath. In his human form he now sat obediently beside his mother. He attentively listened to her as she gave him his instructions. Typhon acknowledged his mother's commands and immediately took off to fly to Cyprus to destroy a woman of great beauty who was named Aphrodite.

***

Zeus swiftly flew Aphrodite to his home at Mount Olympus. Their journey was long, but uneventful and they landed unobserved. Aphrodite dismounted and Zeus morphed into his human form once more. Aphrodite was relieved to be back on the ground, and as exhilarating as flying was, the heights that they flew made her feel a little uncomfortable.

Aphrodite had observed many people from the air and she noted that they were all clothed. She now wanted to learn more, and so she asked Zeus about it. 'I had presumed that you all went about naked, just like I do,' Aphrodite was surprised about their modesty.

'No one goes about naked like you do, Aphrodite. It would cause them too many problems. Oh, do not get me wrong, nudity is not frowned upon it, and often, for the right occasions, it is our standard attire. Mostly, we wear clothing to give other people's imaginations something to think about,' he explained and smiled. He had learned long ago that smiling at the recipient seems to add credence to all of his explanations. Then as an afterthought he added. 'Many females are competitive about their clothing, and others are just practical about what they choose to wear. I'm confident that you'll quickly get the hang of it.'

As Zeus predicted, Aphrodite's arrival at Mount Olympus instantly created massive curiosity. There were gods and goddesses who were going about their normal routines about the marketplace, and they became intrigued when their king returned escorting an unknown beautiful female. They were greeted with friendly banter and good cheer, and Aphrodite observed that Zeus received a warm welcome from the multitudes. Soon a crowd formed behind them as Zeus led them toward his customary public address platform. He alighted and motioned for Aphrodite to step up close to join him.

By now, Zeus's wife, Hera, was outside the family palace and she accompanied by their two adult sons, Hephaestus, and Ares, and their two adult daughters, Eileithyia, and Hebe who was their youngest child.

Zeus was unconcerned with the size of growing audience. He knew they wanted an explanation of who this new woman was, but as protocol would have it, they were respectful enough to wait patiently until Zeus was ready to reveal her identity an also tell them all the details about her. Gods and Goddesses were innately curious.

Zeus took great delight in keeping everybody waiting.

In hushed tones, Zeus gave Aphrodite a quick explanation of the names and roles of gods and goddesses that were now mingling before them. 'That tall woman wearing the red dress, the one with the scowl glaring in our direction, is my wife, Hera. Watch out for her, she is a nasty jealous type. She is the goddess of fidelity, marriage, and childbirth. She oversees the morality of mortal kings and interferes with their dealings with their subjects. She claims that she keeps them in check.'

'Next to her is my oldest son, Hephaestus. When he walks you will notice he has a lame leg. He was permanently injured when he exceeded his position as a young man an he paid a great price for his lesson. Heph is the god of craftsman, and he is an exceptionally capable blacksmith and jeweller. He is worth knowing if you want anything made, especially weapons or jewellery, but he also makes fine furniture.'

Aphrodite smiled. She had observed that many of the beautiful women gathered before them were wearing jewellery, and she liked the idea of having some of her own.

Zeus continued. 'The taller but younger man next to Heph is also my son and his name is, Ares. He is the god of war, and he enjoys a fight and then likes to consummate his victories with vigorous coitus. I suppose he is a bit like me in that way.' Zeus laughed. 'He will definitely be interested in meeting you, but be warned, he is a rascal.'

Aphrodite studied the warrior Ares who returned her gaze with his most alluring smile which she happily reciprocated. She threw him a wink and thought that perhaps he had just blushed a little.

Heph was delighted. He did not see Ares side of the exchange and he thought that her wink and her smile was for him.

'Hebe is wearing a white dress. She is my cup bearer and the goddess of youth. She is totally devoted to me and loves being daddy's little girl,' Zeus beamed.

'Eileithyia, in the blue dress, is more like her mother and she also tends to disapprove of everything I say or do,' Zeus told her. He was laughing. Clearly, he was unperturbed by this strained relationship with his eldest daughter. 'She is also a goddess of childbirth, but lately she seems more intent on preventing any of my liaisons from producing offspring.'

'Over there in the battle dress is Athena. She is also my daughter, but from a different mother. She sees herself of the protector of heroes and has an annoying fondness for helping humans.' Zeus indicated a heavily armoured and weaponised woman who stood alone in the background. 'Her mother Metis and I made her after I defeated my father, Cronus during the war. Metis died soon after Athena was born. Some gods and goddesses claim that I consumed Metis to absorb her powers, but that is not true. Metis, goddess of good counsel gave me much solid advice that I still use today. Athena grew up so fast that many believed she was born an adult.' Zeus laughed at Aphrodite's facial expression. 'It isn't true. Nearly all the gods and goddesses grow quickly into adulthood. You won't see many children here and if you do, they'll be human children.'

Aphrodite nodded. She now planned to befriend the warrior goddess, Athena. She looked fierce and she decided that she could make use of her as a powerful ally.

'Over there are the twins, Artemis and Apollo. They are also my children. Their mother, Leto and I once had a fling and sadly Hera and Eileithyia became absolutely incensed about it. They made Leto give birth to her two babies in separate locations. Leto gave birth to Artemis easily enough, but the poor woman had to travel to Delos to give birth to Apollo nine days later. Her children are fine, but the experience ruined their mother, and she has never forgiven me for what Hera and Eileithyia did to her.' Zeus looked glum.

'You seem to have a lot of children.' Aphrodite concluded.

Zeus laughed. 'That's true. I really do!' he laughed once more. 'I have impressive seed, what else can I say?' he laughed again and still chuckling, he turned to the crowd once more.

'Dionysos is the god of wine, and he enjoys throwing a party. Any excuse for one will do. Does drinking wine affect you?' Zeus queried.

'I have never tried it,' Aphrodite admitted.

'But you have heard of it?' Zeus was surprised.

'Yes, of course,' she replied.

'Be wary of it. We at Mount Olympus tend to consume a lot of it, and many of us have had cause for regret after succumbing to wines powers,' Zeus cautioned.

'As a god, can't you nullify its effect?' Aphrodite was confused.

'What would be the fun of doing that?' He mocked being shocked and then laughed as he resumed his explanations. 'Hermes is the messenger of the gods. He is useful to know, and you can use him for any of your communication and travel needs. He is also great at writing, and he is conversant in many languages. He doesn't know that he is also my son though I believe that he might suspect it.' Zeus looked at Aphrodite indicating that she should not share this knowledge with anyone. She nodded her acknowledgment and so he continued. 'His mother Maia was a lovely lively nymph who was so scared of Hera finding out about us, that she insisted that we had to meet secretly in a cave. Poor girl, she died young, and I never found out how or why.' Zeus looked sad about it. 'She gave birth to him in secret, and Hermes was able to join us here fairly soon after she died.'

'Your crowd is getting restless,' Aphrodite observed.

Zeus nodded that he was aware of it. He turned to face the crowd and in his bellowing voice he announced, 'Everyone, this is Aphrodite.' He then turned to face her. 'Aphrodite, this is everyone.' He cast his extended arm and hand toward those gathered as the Sun God Helios obliged by beaming brighter, lighting up their faces.

Aphrodite was impressed.

'You go and meet the people, and I'll go and deal with my seething wife,' Zeus said as he winced, forced a smile, and then grimaced.

But Aphrodite was not concerned for him. She already knew that she wanted to make alliances, and she particularly wanted to meet a worthy man to have sex with.

***

As soon as he arrived at Cyprus, Typhon flew several times across the island undertaking a full reconnaissance. All his eyes were searching for a beautiful young woman. He swooped low over the four Seasons home, and he next circled the island many times looking for her, but he was without success. He decided to land, and he transformed into his human form to make his way by foot to the structure where the Seasons lived. He secretively studied them for some time, but he eventually concluded that his target was no longer on the island. He was ordered by his mother not to harm or to communicate with the female Seasons, as he was only here to kill the young woman named Aphrodite. So, he quietly withdrew, morphed, and flew back to report to Gaia.

In his human form, Typhon dutifully sat down beside his mother and gave his account. He told her of what he had seen, and his conclusion was that she had departed from the island before he could get there. Gaia was not surprised that Aphrodite was gone. She stood up and turned to face her monstrous child. 'I want you to travel to Mount Olympus,' she instructed. 'In your human form, you will be allowed to enter Mount Olympus to seek out Aphrodite. When you land, you will need to find human clothing as soon as you can. Get dressed, enter the citadel, find her, and kill her. Do this quietly and discreetly. Talk to no-one. It must be as if you were never there. Be cautious of meeting or upsetting Zeus. He has many friends and followers and if they confront you, they may be able to find a way to defeat you whilst you are in your human form.'

'If Zeus challenges me, I will grow my many heads and spit fire and venom onto him. I'll grow my many hands out from my body, and I'll pummel him to death,' Typhon retorted laughing.

'Even in that form, Zeus might find a way to defeat you,' Gaia reiterated kindly. 'You must be clever. First separate Aphrodite from Zeus's protection, and then kill her. Do you understand?'

'I do,' he agreed.

'Go,' Gaia commanded pointing toward his destination.

Once again Typhon's giant wings sprouted and he leapt into the air, and full of purpose, he flew at great speed toward Mount Olympus.

***

Hera did not appreciate her husband's attempt at a kiss, and it landed on her cheekbone near to her ear. She scolded him without reservation. 'Who is this harlot, and why did you bring her to our home?' she demanded.

'Her name is Aphrodite, parentage unknown.' Zeus smiled. 'Don't worry I didn't bed her.' He moved closer to her to try once more to kiss her. This manoeuvre often weakened her resolve.

Hera broke away from Zeus and purposefully marched up to Aphrodite. She wasn't smiling. Aphrodite smiled and held out her hand in greeting. Hera took it in both her hands and held it tightly while she looked deep into Aphrodite's eyes. She said nothing, her face impassive.

Then, without a word of explanation, she released Aphrodite's hand, turned and walked away, motioning to Zeus that he should follow her. When they were out of earshot from the others she said kindly to Zeus. 'She is still a virgin, so I can accept that you did not bed her.'

Zeus's victory smile was short lived.

'Did you try and fail?' Hera sounded condescending.

'No!' Zeus defended. 'I have kept my promise to be faithful to you, my love.'

Hera was not impressed. 'Why did you bring her here to Mount Olympus?' she demanded.

'She was raised by the Horai. Chioné didn't want her to live there anymore, and she even threatened to do her permanent harm.'

'Does Chioné have valid reasons to hurt her?' Hera was suspicious.

'None that I am aware of. Perhaps she is just jealous of her remarkable beauty,' Zeus speculated.

'Is she beautiful? I hadn't noticed,' Hera replied, feigning disinterest.

Zeus sighed. 'Aphrodite is now one of us. Please just deal with it.'

'I'd feel better if she were married. Then her husband would be responsible for her safety and not you. Perhaps we should find her a husband so he can insulate her from unsuitable attention,' Hera decided. Her cold staring eyes penetrated deep into Zeus. She had made certain that he got the message.

***

Typhon managed to arrive unobtrusively on the outskirts of Mount Olympus. He quickly reduced his size and shape to approximate an adult human male. His wings were the last non-human appendages to disappear, which did they did the instant he landed. He was confident that he had arrived unseen by either god or mortal. He hurriedly searched for some clothing to wear, and he approached an isolated farmhouse where he spotted some recently washed men's clothing that was drying in the sunlight. When he was satisfied that he could move about unseen, he removed it from the drying rack, retreated into the undergrowth, and quickly dressed as he adjusted his body size to fit perfectly into the clothing. He next set forth at an urgent pace towards the city gates.

***

As Aphrodite walked through the crowds, she quickly realised that by being raised by three of the Seasons, in the relative isolation of Cyprus, that they had not sufficiently prepared her with the necessary social skills she needed to mingle effectively with these people. She was surprisingly feeling a little nervous. She was naturally fascinated with most of the men, and she was intimidated, intrigued, and aroused all at the same time. She decided the only way to deal with her conflicting emotions, was to confront these men, and learn from her encounters with them. She also wondered about what it would be like to interact with these women. It had occurred to her that many of these men could be in some form of committed relationship with a woman, just like Zeus was, and that the men might be reluctant to enjoy an intimate association with her for fear of subsequent retribution from their female.

Aphrodite did not want to put the women off-side, so she decided she would mingle with all of them She would learn who was with who and work out which of these male gods were available to her.

There was a man that Zeus said was named Ares and she thought he looked interesting. She decided she would start with him and so she nonchalantly walked over to him. When he saw her approaching, his face immediately broke out into a reassuring and welcoming smile. That was fortunate for her, as she had already realised that a man's smile instantly weakened his resistance and made him more compliant.

Another man interceded and she recognised him as Zeus's other son, Hephaestus.

'Forgive me, Aphrodite,' Hephaestus blurted holding out his hand.

'There is nothing to forgive,' she replied with a generous smile taking his hand in hers.

Hephaestus held her hand as if examining it. He brought the back of her hand to his lips and gently kissed it. He then looked at it closely as if measuring it. Finally, he spoke. 'You are to most beautiful woman I have ever seen,' he assured her. 'I can craft jewellery for you that will perfectly match your fingers, wrists, and neck.'

'I think I'd like that, Hephaestus. You'd be my hero,' she told him smiling warmly.

His heartbeat raced and he was now totally captivated by her. She knew his name! He felt totally and deeply in awe of her, and he now wanted to be with her forever. He was so pleased as this was the first time that he had ever felt this way about anyone. He now knew he wanted this feeling to continue forever.

'Heph!'

The summons managed to interrupt his thoughts. Heph turned to see his younger brother pointing to Aphrodite's hand. 'She may want that back,' he advised.

Heph looked at the hand and immediately let go of it. He blushed in embarrassment, and he turned away from the two of them and hastily left the area.

Aphrodite turned to her rescuer. 'Zeus said your name is Ares,' she said conversationally.

'And he told me that your name is Aphrodite,' he replied. 'Sorry about Heph,' he added smiling at his older brother's awkwardness. 'He's somewhat inexperienced for his age.'

'He's sweet,' she replied confidently, her eyes still watching Heph's hurried departure. She then turned back to Ares and studied his form. Liking what she saw she smiled her interest. 'I gather that you are more experienced?'

Ares moved adjusting his stance into what he thought was more manly pose. He wanted to appear strong and confident looking. He examined her face directly seeking her reaction when she looked his way. It seemed that it was positive, and so he smiled enthusiastically at her once more. He then relaxed and composed himself, 'Sweet isn't a word I'd use to describe Heph.'

'How well do you get on with, Zeus?' Aphrodite wanted to establish his relationship to her benefactor.

'Not so good,' he replied shaking his head slightly, surprised at her lack of knowledge.

'Aren't you good friends?' she asked innocently.

'We have as good a friendship as a son can have with his father, I suppose,' he replied. 'He has many children, but he only truly dotes on Hebe.'

'Are any of these women yours?' Aphrodite asked casually looking about the women in their vicinity.

'Are you asking me if I am in a committed relationship?' Ares replied.

Aphrodite continued to look about her.

'No. The nature of my work tends to keep me free and available to enjoy all new worthwhile pleasurable opportunities that present themselves,' he assured her smiling.

'Good,' Aphrodite declared. 'I desire to know you intimately,' she told him whilst placing her hand on his chest. 'Do you know anything about sex?'

He looked at her incredulously. 'This is my lucky day,' he replied.

'Does that mean, that you do?' she was puzzled.

Ares restrained himself from laughing. He did not what to spoil the mood or lose the opportunity to be with this woman. 'It certainly does!' he assured her and then quickly added, 'You name the where, and the when, and I'll be there to show you just how good at sex I am.'

It then occurred to Aphrodite that she did not know where she would be staying. She had presumed Zeus would support her, but after meeting Hera, she was not so sure that that would happen. She needed a place to rest and wash, and more importantly a place to be naked with this man. She had long ago figured out that for gods, and even for humans, that copulation was generally not a spectator activity, so whilst she understood the need for privacy, she had also totally dismissed the need for discretion.

'I am new here, and I have yet to learn about my habitation arrangements. Perhaps you could share your bed with me?' she suggested.

Ares coughed. He looked at his mother from across the courtyard and his face blushed. This was a rare emotion for him, and he was about to reply. 'I'd have to ask my mother,' but he thought this would make him seem immature, so he finally answered in a voice that revealed his embarrassment. 'It would be much better if we could find somewhere else to meet.' Ares looked about him, hopeful of finding a solution.

Athena had been listening to their conversation, and she was amused by Ares's dilemma. She was generally kind toward him and had decided that now was a good time to intercede. 'Perhaps I could keep Aphrodite entertained, while you try to clear a path to a suitable bed chamber,' Athena offered grinning. 'When you are ready, you'll find her at my place.'

Ares blushed once more. He was feeling like a young child and that he was once more at the mercy of women. 'Thanks Athena,' he said. He then added, 'Could we perhaps use your place?

'No.'

He slowly nodded, turned, and walked towards his mother.

Aphrodite and Athena watched him as he walked away. They saw Hera take her son's arm and lead him into their family home. Zeus, Hebe, and Eileithyia dutifully followed them, and the door shut resoundingly behind them.

'Ares is just a boy in a man's body,' Athena sighed. 'Aphrodite. I know a place where we can have a meal, a drink, and some uninterrupted girl talk,' Athena suggested.

'I'd appreciate all three,' Aphrodite smiled in agreement.

From a discreet distance, unobserved by the two women, Hephaestus watched their emerging friendship develop. His eyes followed them as they headed off together.

As they were walking toward a popular eatery, an ugly smelly man approached them. 'Aphrodite!' he yelled in a loud authoritative voice. He looked to the two gorgeous women standing before him, clearly confused as to who he thought he was addressing.

Athena motioned Aphrodite to remain quiet and calm. They stood still as they studied the man, but both said nothing.

'Which one of you is Aphrodite?' the man demanded.

'A gentleman would offer his name before demanding to know ours?' Athena suggested kindly.

The man looked troubled, but he recognised the opportunity to progress his enquiry. 'I am Typhon,' he answered swelling his chest to indicate his strength and importance.

'A gentleman would wash before approaching women and then addressing them in familiar terms,' Athena continued.

The man looked from one to the other. He looked at his arms and then lifted one to his nose and sniffed. Clearly, he could understand the issue as he was surprised by his own stench.

'Um,' Typhon hesitated. 'I will clean up later. Which one of you is Aphrodite?'

'Why don't you clean up now?' Athena suggested. 'Then you can meet us properly and perhaps you could even share a meal with us while we talk. You do look hungry,' Athena suggested, using a tried and tested appeal to this man, via his stomach. 'There is a stream not far from here, and the water is a pleasant temperature at this time of the year.' Athena next motioned toward the path that Typhon should take.

Typhon hesitated. He was here to kill Aphrodite, but these two as yet unidentified women were being kind to him. Perhaps neither of them was Aphrodite, but maybe they might know where she was. He was hungry and so the prospect of washing and sharing a meal with them became an attractive proposition.

'Okay. I will do as you suggest,' Typhon agreed nodding. He then turned and headed toward the path he was gone.

'Who is he?' Aphrodite was concerned why this man was seeking her out.

'I do not know, but I think we should find out before we let him know who you are,' Athena cautioned.

'He stank,' Aphrodite said as they turned and headed for the eatery.

Athena suddenly stopped and held Aphrodite's arm. 'We should go to my palace to eat. Typhon will be looking for us and he might be planning to make a nuisance of himself.'

Athena led Aphrodite through the passageways that took them to her home. The two women entered Athena's abode and they soon found a comfortable room in which to relax, eat, and drink, as they talked about themselves. Aphrodite told Athena the little that she knew about herself. She told her about how she was found by the Seasons and how three of them raised her. She talked about her loves and dislikes, and then completed her account describing her meeting with Zeus, and their journey to Mount Olympus.

Athena spoke about her work. She particularly focused on her role as guardian and mentor to the humans. She loved to make things and enjoyed teasing Hephaestus about her being more skilled than he was, even though she knew it was not true. She told her about her design and creation of both the spinning wheel and the weaving loom. She also enjoyed making her own chariots as she was a skilled wood turner and fitter.

Aphrodite was fascinated. For her, this woman was awe-inspiring. She wanted to know more. 'What about men?' she asked casually.

Athena drew a deep breath and explained. 'I advise many kings and their generals about military strategy. Mostly my involvement has been to dissuade them the use of military force and so I try to facilitate a diplomatic solution to appease their ambitions. I do allow the men their macho military posturing. They do like to dress up in military regalia, and I agree that for many, they look great in a uniform...'

'Have you had many?' Aphrodite interrupted.

Athena laughed. 'Thank the Gods, no!' She smiled at her new friend, now understanding where she was heading to with her questions. 'I choose to remain chaste. I rely on no man, or woman, for my physical pleasures.'

'You were never tempted to try, not even once?' Aphrodite was eager to bed a man. She felt her hunger for copulation growing deeper within her. It was like she was driven by the need to experience it and own it.

'Well,' Athena confided. 'Heph and I came close to "doing it" once. He and I were in his workshop crafting some furniture for my home. We were together and we often worked in close proximity during the assembly stage, and he brushed my leg with his groin. To my surprise I realised he was sporting a massive erection!' she laughed at the memory of it.

'What did you do?' Aphrodite was beyond curious.

'Of course, I was flattered. I knew he loved me, but I had hoped it was a brotherly love and not a romantic, or sexual love. But, typical of all men, show them any kindness or affection, and all they want to do is stick it inside you.'

'Did you let him?' Aphrodite encouraged her to continue.

'I had thought that one day that I would. I thought that perhaps I was ready, that I should learn firsthand what it felt like, but as we arranged ourselves into a workable position, he spilled his seed on my inner thigh.' She sighed. 'My one and only sexual experience was over before it even started.'

'Heph didn't ask you to try again?'

'No. The poor boy was extremely embarrassed. I think he was worried that I might have felt that he was somehow forcing me to do it, because of our friendship. He was not, I mean look at me. No man would ever dare to try forced sex with a warrior with my strength, skills, and battle experience. It would never happen.' Athena paused and looked away in deep reflection. 'I had hoped that our friendship would return to normal, and that we could still work on projects together, but that hasn't happened yet.' She smiled. 'I think Heph is more the marrying kind. He needs a calm patient wife who will be his best friend and guide him gently through the physical acts of love.'

'Then he is not the man for me,' Aphrodite concluded. 'I want an experienced man, one who can bed me and make me feel alive and fabulous. I do not want to be restricted by a burdensome husband. I want males I can have sex with and then dismiss them when they become boring. I want to be able to move onto my next conquest without them getting all upset about it.'

Athena spoke, choosing tactful words. 'Zeus has a reputation for being good at sexual pleasuring. I am surprise he did not suggest showing off his skills and experience with you.'

'At first, when he saw me naked, I could tell that he was aroused and that he wanted to have sex with me. And obviously, I was read to receive him. But just as we were starting, he just stopped. And then, he pushed me away.'

Athena looked puzzled.

'It seemed that his thingy could not get hard, and so I asked him about that, but he just said something about remaining faithful to his wife and keeping a promise that he had only just made. I did not understand it very much, but without a stiff thingy, I knew sex with him was not going to happen.'

'I would keep the details of Zeus's flaccid penis out of any future conversations that you have with anyone. Zeus would learn of it and he might become embarrassed. He would become furious, as it would send a terrible message about him to everyone in his kingdom.'

'So, it never happened?'

'It never happened,' agreed Athena nodding.

'Nothing at all happened,' Aphrodite concluded. She studied Athena and then added. 'Nothing was even attempted.'

'Only that Zeus was faithful to his wife and a perfect gentleman to you.' Athena drew in a deep breath and continued. 'Hera tends to frown on infidelity. Especially her husbands. Be choosy about who you copulate with, or she will cause trouble for you,' Athena advised. She looked at her new companion with mixed emotion. She had hoped they would become close friends, but now, she was not so sure.

***

Hera beckoned Zeus and her four adult children to follow her to the dinner table for their family meal. Their routine was one that they had practiced many times over the years, although it was lately becoming less frequent that all six of the family members were present at the same mealtime. Food and wine were being served by their most trusted servants as the six sat at the large, spectacularly ornate hand carved, and highly polished wooden rectangular table. It was one that Heph had hand crafted and gifted to the family. Zeus and Hera sat in their regular positions at each end. As was custom, Hebe and Ares sat closest to their father, whilst Eileithyia and Hephaestus sat nearer to their mother.

Ares's face betrayed that he was in deep thought. As a God of War, he was often away and involved with the uglier aspects of the mortal's military campaigns. It was his role to give courage to the men and enable them to commit acts of savagery during the battle so that they should prevail. His physical strength, skills with weaponry, and his resilience and determination during the battle were inspirational. He was devious, cunning, and totally flexible, and he reacted quickly to the changing tide during any conflict. He was a strategist, and his advice was often sought out by kings and generals before any significant campaign. During these dark and troubling times for the numerous warring kingdoms, it meant that their campaigns kept him away from his family for much of his time. Ares did not have many friends, or followers, but this did not bother him too much. He looked at his mother. She claimed to love him unconditionally, but he knew that was not true. He believed that his father, Zeus did not like him at all. Their tensions between them were exacerbated whenever Zeus felt he had supported the wrong side or had gone too far with his brutality. Ares pondered Aphrodite's offer and was now in deep thought contemplating to practicalities of bedding Aphrodite within the family home. He was trying to solve the question of discretion yet fearing parental wrath over enacting his plans. He also worried about of missing out on this delicious opportunity. He laughed inwardly to himself as he found his predicament funny; him worrying about something as basic as sex. He conceded that Aphrodite was probably the most luscious, beautiful, and desirable woman that he would ever meet, and he now desperately wanted to be the first man to have sex with her. In his mind, he could picture her naked, and...'

'Ares!' Zeus interrupted his son's fantasy.

'Answer your father,' Hera said motioning to her son.

Ares looked confused.

'Have you finished with the apple sauce?' Zeus demanded, 'Could you please pass it to me?' He was clearly frustrated with his son's inattention.

Ares looked at the table and then spotted the dish with the apple sauce next to his plate. It was his father's favourite. 'Yes, of course.' He passed the bowl toward his father who grunted in acknowledgement.

Eileithyia's pondering at the dinner table was much different from Ares. She was the goddess of childbirth. Her mother oversaw her training and granted her powers. Hera herself was responsible for many activities that included fidelity and marriage, so she encouraged Eileithyia to focus on childbirth. She could ease the pain and duration of childbirth for any woman that pleased her. But she could also prolong the agony of childbirth to any woman that did not. She decided she would monitor her father's relationship with Aphrodite, though she conceded that she would be powerless to prevent a liaison between them if he chose to have one. Perhaps, Ares would beat their father into Aphrodite's bed. She thought that that would be funny, and she inwardly smiled.

Eileithyia intensely disliked both her brothers, and she often smirked at any punishments dealt toward them. She took some pleasure when her siblings were receiving a scolding and she actively encouraged punishments toward them from their parents. She had always sought both of her parent's approval and their praise. This she received in abundance from her mother, but sadly for her, not from her father, who treated her with indifference. Hebe had that aspect of his affections monopolised. She had always openly disapproved of her father's infidelities but had long ago given up on trying to dissuade him from being unfaithful to her mother.

Ares interrupted her thoughts. 'I am thinking of moving out of the palace,' he said to no-one specifically. 'I think it is time that I got a place of my own.'

'Good,' she said nodding, and she was a little surprised at her own enthusiasm for his announcement but proceeded anyway. 'That's a great plan,' Eileithyia quickly added. 'I will... help you pack,' she offered with a smile.

'But why, darling? You're so happy here, and you want for nothing,' Hera countered indicating the food and the palace.

Zeus however was quick to defend his son's decision. 'I fully agree with Ares. I agree that it is about time that he manned up and went out on his own. Every child should build their own nest when they reach adulthood. It builds character and independence. I will even help you find a suitable place,' he offered smiling generously at his son.

'Er, thanks,' Ares replied cautiously. His father often had an ulterior motive when quickly agreeing with him.

Hera also looked suspiciously at her husband. She also knew that Zeus often had a hidden agenda when readily agreeing with any of their children's plans.

Hephaestus listened to the exchange with intrigue. He had also been busy with his own thoughts during the moments preceding

Ares's announcement. He was always at odds with family life and generally with the world. He was respected as a craftsman, but not as a man. His lame leg made him the target of much public ridicule. After, when they wanted something crafted by him, they privately apologised for their publicly mean behaviour toward him. He knew the form, and mostly he chose to ignor their admonishments. He too had desires for Aphrodite. If only he could capture Aphrodite's love and perhaps romance her to the point when she would want to marry him. He would become the envy of all those gods that had tormented him. He felt confident that she was the one for him, and he imagined that their union would make them both very happy in so many ways. He could not wait for this meal to conclude, so that he could go out to locate, and hopefully seduce Aphrodite convincingly. He then decided he needed to hurry before some other man beat him to her. He reached out and served himself more food which he ate with gusto, surprising his father who often complained at how slow he was at eating during their shared family mealtimes.

'I am thinking of moving out also,' Hephaestus announced through mouthfuls. He appeared to be following his younger brother's lead.

'Good for you son. A man should have a palace of his own,' Zeus said encouragingly.

'But where will you move to?' Hera wanted to show her immediate concern, but she inwardly knew that she was also relieved. Heph's "Stuff" took up a lot of room and it always looked untidy to her. Often, she found items that he had salvaged, that clearly did not belong in her home. She was tired of reminding him that he had a workshop and that he should store his treasures away from the palace, but her pleas were most often ignored.

'There is enough room above my workshop. I can clear some space for my bed and for my clothes.' Heph explained calmly whilst trying to sound convincing. His mother was famous for pretending to be concerned, and then messing about with his plans, just because she could.

'You will never attract a suitable woman to marry you if you live above your workshop,' Hera decided. 'You are far better off staying here.'

'I think he should go,' Zeus often sided with Heph. He was never going to be a challenge to his authority. Ares might be trouble one day, but he could not imagine Heph causing him too much grief. Heph had real value. He is a fine and respected craftsman, and he had supplied him an unlimited supply of powerful and high-quality lightning bolts, among other things. They had shared a trouble past, but that was now behind them. For the most, he was also a reasonable person to deal with.

Hebe had also been lost in her own thoughts. She liked to romanticise about being married to a big, strong, handsome, responsible, respectable man, who would worship her and protect and love her. She accepted that it would be better if he also had her parent's approval. She did not like Eileithyia for her tell-tale ways, and she certainly did not approve of Ares violent ways. She loved Heph because he was always kind to her and gave her, "especially for her," surprises of hand-crafted gifts, which were spectacular, thoughtful, and made with big brotherly love. Hebe adored her father and she looked up to him as a role model for all other men, and therefore had an idea of what potential husbands should do to emulate him. Being her daddy's cup bearer for special occasions was a doddle, and so she also took a special interest in the affairs of mortal youths. She knew she would not be leaving the family home for a long time. She sat still, smiled, and was content with her own thoughts.

'Will you help me pack little sister?' Heph asked her.

'Only, if I can have your room. It is bigger than mine,' Hebe replied smiling at the thought of having all that extra space.

'Sure,' Heph conceded. He had always known that she had wanted it and she had often lamented about how lucky he was to have so much space. Of all the rooms that were allocated to the children, it also had the best views of the countryside. He would miss his little sister and he hoped she would visit him often at his workshop.

'I am already planning on how to redecorate my new room,' Hebe announced with a smile. She already had a vision of what her new bedroom would look like, and it pleased her.

'So, it's decided then?' Hera was not impressed. 'Both my sons are leaving me.'

'Both our sons are old enough to make their own decisions,' Zeus reminded his wife. 'Just remember boys, leaving the family home is a one-way trip.' He looked at them both in turn with his serious facial expression.

They both nodded their understanding and agreement.

Zeus had wanted this day to come for a long time. Having four adult children living at home really cramped him. Hera was always complaining about petty things about them. If they would all leave home, she might spend less time complaining and more of her time pleasing him. She could also focus on more important aspects of her role as goddess for mortal kings and their kingdoms. It would be good for her to get out of the house more often.

Zeus next wondered about Aphrodite's current activities. He had already concluded that he would not get the opportunity to bed her any-time soon, maybe never at all. He could also tell that both of his sons were also interested in bedding her. He thought that he would enjoy watching how that competition would play out. And, if one of them married her, then he would be frequently visiting their home, and that would be nice, especially if she continued to walk about naked. Beautiful naked women never lost their appeal. Zeus smiled broadly, but then quickly corrected the mistake. He checked to see if Hera had noticed his smile, but fortunately she was busily interrogating Ares on his plans. Hera had a nasty habit of correctly interpreting his thoughts, especially when he was smiling.

'I'll want to check out your new home as I will want to make sure it is adequate for you. I will also arrange for some staff to clean and cook for you,' Hera explained to Ares reassuringly. She then gave him that motherly look as if she wanted to make sure that he understood that she was only concerned for his own best interests.

'Yes mother,' Ares agreed capitulating with his winning smile. He had learned as a boy not to argue with mother, but to just quickly agree with her. It removed any potential annoying struggle between them for the things he really wanted, and what his mother would actually allow. He would always do as he pleased, but it would certainly be easier when he was free from her scrutiny.

Before her son's pronouncement Hera had also been thinking. She had felt that for a long time she had been neglecting her godly responsibilities toward the mortal kings and their kingdoms that they ruled. Perhaps this would be a good time to revisit them She would reassert her influence over them, their plans, and their destinies. Besides, when Zeus decreed that he supported their son's decisions about leaving home, there was little point having a protracted debate with him about it, as he always won in the end. She remembered how he persisted in wooing her, after she had so many times rejected his advances. She had no intention of becoming his wife number seven, but he had tricked her into falling in love with him by presenting himself as a bedraggled cuckoo bird. She had felt overwhelming sympathy for the poor creature, and so she had towelled him dry, and then held him between her exposed breasts to give him warmth. He then slowly changed into his human form and proceeded to kiss her neck and then continued down her body in order to pleasure her completely. She was inexperienced to the art of lovemaking but discovered that she greatly enjoyed these new sensations immensely. Later, the memory of the experience shamed her, and so to neutralise her embarrassment of being treated in this way, she conceded to marry him. She also quickly learned that by becoming his wife, it greatly enhanced all her powers and privileges. This was the aspect of their marriage that she appreciated considerably.

Being the goddess of fidelity was always a challenge for Hera, especially considering that her husband was famous for being unfaithful. His dalliances were a constant source of agitation for her. Zeus being the king of the gods did not help her mission either. Fortunately, gods and mortals alike feared them too much to mock them openly for the hypocrisy that was so obvious in their relationship.

Their family meal was now finished, and servants were clearing away the rest of the food and were removing the soiled crockery and cutlery. As was the household custom, the amphora of wine and the wine cups remained on the table until after all the diners had left.

'Thank the gods for the wonderful meal.' Ares had made his traditional praise to leave the table without remonstration. He stood, walked over and kissed his mother's cheek, and then left the room.

Heph stood as he decided that he was also ready to leave. 'Thank you, gods, for all these earthly provisions.' He too smiled, performed a curt wave to all, turned and exited.

Zeus yawned and stretched then scratched his bearded face. 'As king of the gods, I guess I get to thank myself,' and then chuckled at his own joke. No-one laughed as he said it repeatedly.

Hebe stood up, hugged her father, and kissed him on the cheek. 'Thank you, daddy,' she said as she left the room.

'Eileithyia, would you mind leaving also?' I would like a private word with your father,' Hera asked her calmly. Eileithyia looked concerned at both her parents, but obediently rose from her chair. Without a word she quietly walked toward the passageway that led to her own bedroom.

'Yes, my love, my flower, my dove... my queen,' Zeus believed he was practiced at diffusing potential conflict. He held up his wine cup in friendly salute, smiled, and then drank.

'All three of you are plotting on how to bed Aphrodite,' Hera decided.

'Not me,' Zeus defended. 'But I agree that you are correct about Heph and Ares and their plans for her. It's obvious to me that they both have lust on their minds.' He winked at his wife who was not impressed.

Hera sighed. 'I actually only care if you have plans to bed her, as you know I forbid it,' Hera warned.

'Okay, I won't,' Zeus conceded quickly. He inwardly shrugged. There were plenty of other women to have his fun with. It was safer to do so with ones that Hera did not know about. He now decided that he was happy enough to refrain from being with her. 'What about Heph and Ares?'

'I don't care if they do have sex with her. I do not want either of them marrying her. I really do not want her in my life. If she were to become our daughter in-law then she would be visiting us, here, in our home, and I just know that she'll continue to have a tempting influence over you.'

'I had not thought of that,' Zeus lied.

***

Heph and Ares left their family home at about the same time, but from different exits. It was now dark outside, and the olive oil fire lamps were now lit for the benefit of night-time pedestrians. Both men wormed their respective ways through the maze that made up the streets and passageways of Mount Olympus. The lamps created flickering ghostly shadow movements on the walls and doorways that lined the streets. Both brothers were experienced with the layout, and both men were now desperately seeking out the same person, Aphrodite. They also knew that they would find her in the company of Athena, and so each headed in the general direction of Athena's home on the assumption that she would be there.

Ares had thought it through. His plan was to seduce Aphrodite with his manliness, and then convince her that the notion of any available bed was a suitable assignation for their mutually desired coitus. Given her previous predilection for copulation, he felt that she would not take too much convincing. At least he hoped that she did not. Ares also knew that he often thought cleverer than he actually spoke, so he was rehearsing his pitch as he hastily progressed toward her. As he turned a corner he bumped forcibly into another person. 'I am so sorry,' Ares spluttered. 'I was lost in thought and didn't see you in the darkness.'

Typhon picked himself up and dusted himself off, acutely aware that he really should not be attracting too much attention to himself, considering his real purpose for being here. 'That is quite all right,' he reassured his unintentional assailant whilst performing a polite bow. 'I was in haste myself, and I should have looked where I was going and avoided you,' he added and then forced a curt laugh.

Ares looked at the stranger. 'You are new here, aren't you?'

'I am,' Typhon replied. He decided it was best to stick to the truth as much as possible. 'I seek a beautiful woman. Maybe you can help me? Her name is Aphrodite.'

'Such a coincidence!' Ares was pleased. 'I too seek Aphrodite.' Then in a hushed voice he added. 'We have a secret agreement to indulge in an indiscreet rendezvous.'

'Don't you mean, "a discreet rendezvous?"' Typhon corrected.

'Whatever,' Ares countered. He no longer wanted to be helpful to this stranger. 'I must haste.' he explained as he turned to leave.

'I am sorry, but I don't know your name,' Typhon called out stopping him short.

Ares turned back to the man. 'I am Ares.'

'I have personal business with her, but I don't know what she looks like, or where she lives. May I follow you Ares?' Typhon asked in his most hapless voice.

'Is your business with her romantic?'

'No.'

'Well…' Ares hesitated as he considered the request. He did not like competition. 'Perhaps if you told me where you were staying, I could send her to meet with you when we have finished our own rendezvous…,' he suggested.

'How will I know it is her?' Typhon was becoming desperate. He needed to complete his mission and leave Mount Olympus before Zeus learned of his presence.

'Well to begin with, she is the most beautiful woman of all time. Her skin is perfect, her lips are soft and moist, and her hair is golden brown. I tell you, to meet her, is to fall in love with her. I am sorry my friend, but I am desperate to be with her, so tell me your name and I will apprise her of your need to meet with her.'

Typhon felt he was running out of options. 'My name is Typhon and I have an important message for her from her mother.'

'Her mother. Sounds important. I'll be sure to tell her,' Ares promised, and then he broke into a knowing grin. 'I will tell you what I will do. If she is not too exhausted, I will send her to meet you in the vestibule of the "Laughing Amphorae",' he laughed.

Typhon correctly assumed that the "Laughing Amphorae," was a local drinking establishment. 'I look forward to it, thank you kind sir,' he said performing another small bow. 'I hope you get to enjoy your indiscretion.'

'No, no, my name is Ares. I am Zeus's son.' Ares smiled and patted Typhon's shoulder with newfound affection. He waved a farewell and then continued his journey to Athena's palace, and he hoped Aphrodite would still be there with her.

Typhon followed Ares at a prudent distance. He was relieved that he was making no effort to be quiet and that he showed no concern about being followed. They were moving at a hurried pace when suddenly he collided headfirst into yet another night-time wanderer. This time, he was first to apologise. 'I am so sorry,' he insisted to the stranger.

'I was in haste myself,' Heph replied. 'Are you okay?' he asked in concern.

'I am fine, thank you.' Then Typhon realised that Ares was long gone. 'Ah, bother!' He looked about them for some clue as which way to go.

'Have you lost someone?' Heph was concerned.

'My friend,' Typhon exclaimed. 'I am new in town, and I really don't know my way around yet. We have been drinking at the "Laughing Amphorae," and now I have lost my way to my sister's place. That drunken wastrel hasn't even realised that he has left me behind,' Typhon complained.

'Who is your sister, what is her name? Perhaps I can show you the way.' Heph offered wanting to be helpful.

'A beautiful young woman. Her name is, Aphrodite. Perhaps you know off her?' Typhon asked hopefully.

'Aphrodite is your sister!' Heph was delighted to meet the man who might one day be his brother-in-law. 'Yes, I do, most decidedly,' he assured Typhon. 'As a matter of fact, I am on my way to meet with her to make my proposal.'

'Proposal?' Typhon was confused.

'Of marriage of course,' Heph added and grinned happily, confident of his plan.

'You are talking about, Aphrodite, aren't you?' Typhon was confused.

'She is the most delightful, beautiful, caring, and loving goddess of all time,' Heph said dreamily. 'She is the one and only for me, she is my, Aphrodite.'

'Does she have many other suitors?' Typhon queried. He was now becoming concerned for the rationality of his goals. Aphrodite may be too well accompanied for a discrete assassination.

'Too many to count, of that I am certain,' Heph replied, and his face dropped gloomily.

'I shall tell her of your kindness and chivalry, and I will recommend you to her. She is well disposed to listen to the advice of her elder brother,' Typhon assured him with a bow.

Heph grinned happily at making this new worthwhile alliance. 'My name is Heph,' he introduced and extended his hand.

Typhon accepted the handshake and smiled benevolently. 'I am known as Typhon.'

'Come with me and we'll find her together,' Heph motioned as he invited his new friend to the journey.

Typhon did not care if they happened on Aphrodite during her copulation with Ares. He did not care about the negative impact that witnessing their sexual union would have on Heph. He just needed to locate Aphrodite, kill her, and quickly depart Mount Olympus, all before Zeus became aware of his presence. They walked together in relative silence, each with their own thoughts.

Heph was thinking about the lack of family resemblance between sister and brother when Typhon spoke.

'Do you know, Ares?' Typhon asked breaking the silence.

'Yes. He's my younger brother,' Heph replied.

Typhon hid his knowing smile in the shadows. They approached Athena's palace with some speed and as they neared the front door they almost bumped into Ares.

'What are you doing here?' Heph demanded. He was clearly troubled by his brother's presence.

'Aphrodite asked me to meet with her tonight.' Ares was annoyed with his brother's frequent anxiety.

'Is Aphrodite in this building?' Typhon asked.

'Yes,' the brothers chorused.

'She is with Athena,' Heph explained.

'I am lucky to have you as my guide,' Typhon smiled at his benefactor.

'Hey!' I thought I told you that I'll send Aphrodite to meet you when she was ready,' Ares confronted the stranger.

Heph was confused. 'I am here to see Aphrodite for a romantic matter.'

'So am I!' Ares countered.

'Your romantic matters only involve having sex!' Heph accused.

'It's the same thing!' Ares corrected his brother's misconception.

'I am here for love,' Heph retorted. 'I plan to marry Aphrodite.'

'Excuse me. But I must deliver an urgent message to Aphrodite from her mother,' Typhon interjected.

'Just you wait a moment; I am dealing with my brother,' Ares pushed Typhon aside.

'Hey! Don't you push him. That's Typhon, Aphrodite's brother. He'll be my brother-in-law one day.'

'Aphrodite! Marry you?' Ares was incredulous.

'Yes! Why wouldn't she?!'

'Because you're ugly, old, lame, and impotent!' Ares yelled back.

Heph was suddenly enraged. He shrieked and swung the first of many punches that would fly between them. The brothers had been fighting with each other from early in their childhood. Ares usually won, and there was rarely any lasting damage. Ares knew how to restrain his violent tendencies, as he realised there would be devastating family consequences for inflicting permanent injury on his weaker, less skilled brother. Their father enjoyed watching them fight, and he never discouraged them for settling their differences in this way. Their mother on the other hand, would intercede to safeguard both her sons, and she would quickly intercede if she caught them engaged in any physical conflict.

As many of their punches made their mark, the two brothers fell to the ground wrestling for the upper hand. Suddenly, the doors from Athena's home burst open and Athena and Aphrodite emerged as they had become intrigued by all the commotion.

Zeus had also arrived, but he stood quietly in the background to enjoy his son's skirmish. He had been alerted to the commotion by his staff, and fearing for Aphrodite, he had rushed to Athena's home. When he recognised that it was only his two sons locked in a tussle, he assumed it was their mutual amorous intentions towards Aphrodite that had triggered the fighting. He had predictably decided to hold back and watch the fun.

Hera suddenly appeared next to him. Zeus was initially startled, but he did his best not to show it. 'Our sons are fighting over a woman,' he explained to his wife, trying hopefully to dismiss it as a trifle.

'You must be so proud. I see that you're doing your usual nothing to stop them,' Hera observed.

Zeus did not detect the predictable disappointment in her voice. Maybe she was becoming more accepting of the ways of her sons, and how they instinctively chose to resolve their differences.

'I assume that it is safe to conclude that it is Aphrodite that they are fighting over,' Hera observed.

'Athena would never...' Zeus began to explain.

'No, she would not,' Hera rebuffed.

By this time Ares had his brother in a headlock and Heph was punching him ineffectively, trying to force him to let him go.

'Do you want me to...?' Zeus indicated their sons as he looked at Hera, unable to gauge her mood.

'No,' she replied as she shook her head. 'It'll end soon enough and then I'll speak with them myself.'

Zeus winced. Her remonstrations would cause their sons more pain and anguish than any of their fights would inflict.

Typhon now turned to the two women who were distracted by the fight. 'Aphrodite? he asked politely.

'Yes,' the beautiful woman turned to look at him as she replied.

'I am Typhon. We met earlier...'

'I remember you. Athena told you to wash. My, you do look, and smell, so much nicer,' she complimented. Aphrodite then had a clever idea on how to stop the fighting. She went up to Typhon and hugged him and then kissed him fully on the lips. Her hand drifted downward as she sought out his genitals in order to arouse him. She sensed the calm behind her, and so she turned her head to discover that the fighting had indeed stopped. She broke from the embrace and smiled warmly at her astonished audience.

Typhon sighed audibly. He too was now deeply in love with Aphrodite, and he felt wonderful. He knew he could no longer kill her, as he now had to have this woman as his lover. He urgently wanted to express his passion for her, but he was also aware that everyone was watching them.

Ares was confused as he thought Typhon was a simple messenger from Aphrodite's mother. Heph was devastated, as he had planned to marry Aphrodite, and he believed he had her brother's support, now she was kissing him with an intimate lover's kiss. Hera was angry about both her son's behaviour. Zeus was concerned about this stranger's presence at Mount Olympus, so he stepped forward to ask questions. He wanted to know who he was, and why he was here.

Athena was also confused. Why did Aphrodite kiss this stranger and what were Hera, Heph, Ares, and Zeus, all doing outside her home at this hour? Only Aphrodite seemed pleased. She now had four males competing for her affections, and all the attention was on her, as it should be.

'Who are you?' Zeus bellowed his demand.

'His name is Typhon, and he is Aphrodite's brother,' Heph announced.

'I don't have a brother,' Aphrodite corrected. She examined him and then moved away, concerned about the assertion.

'Aphrodite, I will admit that at first I had some unsavoury intentions toward you,' Typhon started to explain. He then turned to face the others and continued to clarify his position, 'As it turns out, I am now wanting her for an entirely different reason.' He looked fondly at Aphrodite once more and smiled with his arms extended in a submissive stance. He then descended to one knee. 'The warmth of your passionate embrace has led me to realise that I could never kill you, Aphrodite, as I now truly love you and desire you unconditionally.'

'Kill me!' Aphrodite was outraged.

'Love her?' Heph was dismayed.

'Do you call that, passion!' Ares snorted in disbelief. He was grinning at the absurdity of what he was hearing and motioned to Athena who shook her head totally dismayed by the proceedings.

Zeus, however, drew upon his sword and was now preparing to permanently dispose of this intruder. Ares nodded to his father, and he flexed his muscles. Athena unsheathed her sword and now held it before her in an attack posture.

Aphrodite withdrew, she moved closer to the door and closer to the relative safety of Athena's home.

Heph ran away.

Typhon realising his predicament, began transforming once more into his monstrous form. His body quickly expanded, and his muscles bulged as his shoulders and neck sprouted a multitude of snake and dragon heads. They immediately prepared to launch venom and fire bolts at his attackers. From his torso, he grew numerous arms with clenched fists which he now swung out viciously at his combatants.

The three warriors skilfully worked together in response to the threat. Zeus accurately hurled his lightning bolts that deflected the heads before they could launch their projectiles. Many heads burned and became cauterised. Athena swung her sword and cut a deep wound in the monsters left leg calf muscle. Ares dived feet first at the monster's shin bone on his right leg, and he kicked it with all his might splintering the bone. He next swung his foot upward and he kicked hard into the monster's expanding testes, and Typhon howled in agony.

As the monster was being attacked from three sides, Heph returned carrying a giant coil of razor-sharp spring wire. It was a new device of his own invention. He gave the handle of one end to Zeus who immediately understood what to do with it. Heph then ran in a wide circle around the monster. As he neared his brother, he passed the coil on to Ares who immediately ran toward Zeus, quickly completing the wire circle entrapping Typhon. Zeus next passed his handle on to Ares, who continued to run toward Heph, as Zeus then took the coil and speedily ran the other way around the monster. In this way, the three men circled Typhon several times, further engulfing him in the wires grip.

Athena continued slashing the monster with her sword, piercing the flesh which now oozed blood. Typhon cried out in agony and looked genuinely terrified.

The more Typhon struggled, the tighter the spring wire coil held him in its grip. He suddenly stopped struggling as he was beginning to understand the nature of his predicament. He then started to decrease his body mass in an effort to become released from the wire. As Typhon shrank, the wire coil contracted and continued to tighten around him. Typhon remained trapped within the coils . He suddenly remembered his wings and found that he could still grow them through the gaps in the wires embrace. They were soon fully formed, and he was able to leap into the air and fly away from his attackers and flee to safety.

Ares started to cheer but Zeus cut him short. 'This isn't a victory,' he admonished his son.

'But the monster withdraws!' Ares exclaimed excitedly pointing at Typhon's fading form. 'We have defeated him.'

'We only scared him off, that's all.'

'He would not dare return.'

'He might,' speculated Hephaestus.

'He said he was here to kill me,' Aphrodite said clearly concerned. She hadn't anticipated becoming the target of an assassin.

Hera now moved forward. She had hidden behind the corner of a building watching everything. She addressed Aphrodite. 'Do you have many enemies?'

'None that I am aware of,' Aphrodite defended. 'Except for maybe, Chioné.'

'She is in the past,' Zeus dismissed the assertion.

'Enemies are easy to make. I have many of them, who cares?' Ares concluded.

'Athena, what do you think?' Zeus asked the wise warrior woman.

'We know very little about our new arrival,' she said as she stepped closer and studied Aphrodite. 'It is difficult to say anything about her with any confidence.' She turned to the others and continued. 'We must assume that Typhon is still be only a youth, or we would have heard about a monster like him before now. I would speculate that he is a creation of Gaia. She has manifested many monsters into this world, and Typhon fits the type. I would therefore assume that it was Gaia that sent Typhon here to kill Aphrodite.'

'So, why didn't he? He had the opportunity to kill her when we were all distracted by these two fighting idiots,' Hera asked as she referred to her sons.

'He said, he had fallen in love with me,' Aphrodite said and was perplexed.

'Did you kiss him or in any any way sexually arouse him,' Athena observed.

'I did. But I only did it to distract these two enough to stop their fighting,' Aphrodite defended pointing at both Hephaestus and Ares.

Zeus laughed. 'Aphrodite, Aphrodite. You have been with us for less than a day, and you already have three men fighting over you. I shall be watching your progress through our society with great interest.'

'As will I,' Hera added.

'Shall we adjourn into my home for refreshment?' Athena invited them all into her palace. 'I think we should discuss Typhon some more. I believe he will return and that we should prepare for it.'

They followed Athena into her home and into a communal room filled with recliners and tables that were covered with fruits, cakes, cured meats, cheeses, and amphora of wine.

'You were expecting us?' Hera commented.

'My staff are both organised and discreet,' Athena explained as she bowed toward her guests.

'But there are no wine cups,' Zeus observed.

'I will arrange some,' Athena conceded and turned to leave the room.

'I am going to freshen up. All this excitement is too much for me.' Aphrodite also moved to leave the room.

'Are you Athena's house guest?' Hera called.

'She said I should stay here for as long as I like,' Aphrodite answered smiling as she left the room.

Ares yawned and stretched. 'Thank Athena for me, but my leg is sore from the battle.' He rubbed his leg and winced in exaggerated pain. 'I am going home to rest.' He also left the room and headed for the front door.

'I must speak with Aphrodite,' Heph told his parents and then he too left the room but walked in the direction of Aphrodite's guest room.

Heph knew that if he wanted to be the first to seduce Aphrodite then he had to move quickly. He knew that his brother was planning to bed her, but he was also confident that as soon as Areas learned that he and Aphrodite were betrothed, that even Ares would respect their marriage plans, fidelity, and that he would withdraw. Time was of the essence.

The door to her room was open and he looked in. Aphrodite was naked and his heart pounded with the excitement of it all. She was stunning and his image of the perfectly formed woman. He was surely the luckiest man alive to have fallen in love with this magnificently beautiful woman.

'Come in Heph,' Aphrodite invited. 'Athena has lent me some of her clothing and I am just deciding what to wear.' She held up some clothing and was not the least bit concerned being seen naked.

'I think you should stay just as you are,' Heph suggested hopefully. 'You look magnificent.'

'Why thank you Heph, you are sweet. I do prefer to be nude. She smiled. 'And I think so would your father and Ares. But I think Athena would frown, and your mother would certainly disapprove.'

Heph quickly dropped to one knee. 'Aphrodite,' he started unsteadily. 'I love you, and I'll always love you. I have a home for you, and I would be honoured, and so proud, if you would consent to become my wife.'

Aphrodite stopped dressing midway. She was surprised by this development. She hesitated with her response. She stood upright and the gown fell down and over her waist. She stood still and now looked at him with renewed interest. She knew that if she wanted to remain at Mount Olympus, she needed a permanent home and she knew that Heph had one. Also, she had learned that he was a skilled craftsman and that he could make her jewellery and other items that she might like to possess. The thought of sharing his bed did not excite her at all, but then, it was not distasteful either. Marrying this man would allow her to stay at Mount Olympus in defiance of his mother who had made it perfectly clear that she wanted her to leave. It would also please Zeus, of that she was certain, and it would be supported by Athena who was already showing signs of disapproving her immodest ways. Marrying this man had much merit.

She walked over to Hephaestus who was still down on one knee. She pressed his head into her breasts and held him lovingly. She then guided him up to his feet and kissed him gently on the lips. 'My dear Heph.' she said looking deeply into his eyes. 'You are so sweet, and I love you for your proposal. I am new to Mount Olympus, and I must quickly adjust to my future life here. I think your proposal holds much merit, and so I now ask that you to be true to me whilst I give it my most honest consideration.' She then smiled her smile that she now knew had an entrancing effect on men. 'Will you give me some time to reach the best decision for both of us?' She kissed him once more to seal the arrangement.

Heph's heart leapt with joy. She had consented to consider marrying him when he had feared outright rejection. Of course, he would give her time. She had only just arrived at Mount Olympus and needed time to settle. 'Yes, of course,' he stumbled out his response.

'Now I want you to go back to the others. Please promise me that you'll wait for my answer before you tell the others what you have proposed.'

'I will,' he started but then hesitated. 'I mean, I will return to the others, but I won't discuss our plans with anyone.'

'You are a good man.' She leaned forward and kissed him lightly once more.

With his heart pounding with happiness, Hephaestus left her room and returned to the communal room.

Then Ares entered Aphrodite's room. 'I thought he'd never leave.' He looked in the direction of his departing brother.

'Hello Ares. I was hoping that you'd visit me.' Aphrodite smiled appreciatively as her clothing fell to the floor.

Ares recognised this invitation and quickly followed her example. He was soon naked, and his member was already solidly erect. He could tell Aphrodite was delighted to see it and was already laid back on the bed beckoning him to bring it to her. He did not need any additional encouragement. She stretched her legs wide apart, bent her knees as she guided him deep inside her. Their passion and lust for each other was extreme, and after grinding each other for many exquisite moments, they each gave off a muffled cry of ecstasy as they both climaxed in orgasmic delight. They collapsed next to each other panting, both exhausted and spent.

'Well done on keeping your voice low,' Ares complimented her. He leaned over to give her a congratulatory kiss. 'It would not be good for my parents to hear us.'

She kissed him passionately. 'Thank you for awakening my womanhood,' she purred.

He kissed her as he caressed her sex. 'Thank you for allowing me too. I feel most honoured.'

His strokes were loving and gentle. She felt herself becoming aroused once more. She reached for his member and was delighted to discover that he was already aroused. She moved to open her legs once more and their second frenzied coitus was also mutually pleasurable.

While their breathing slowly returned to normal, Ares made his suggestion. 'They believe that I have gone home. They are not expecting to see me again tonight. Perhaps, I could stay here, with you?' he suggested with his practiced facial expression of hopefulness. He blinked rapidly.

Aphrodite smiled and she looked thoughtfully at Ares and considered his suggestion. She kissed him lightly. 'Given that your father is the King of the Gods, and he did, along with your brilliant fighting skills, just save me from Typhon, and with your mother here, and my host expecting me to return, I should really go and spend some time with them.'

Ares nodded his reluctant agreement. 'I will enjoy myself watching you bathe, and then I'll return home.'

'Bathe?' She queried.

'If you don't, they will smell our passion as soon as you enter the room. For now, I think the truth of our pleasures, should remain ours alone.'

Aphrodite considered his advice. She nodded mostly to herself. She thought that it would be better for Heph to think that she might actually marry him. When his parents learned of their engagement, it should take the pressure off Hera's looming hostility that she constantly displayed toward her. She would have Zeus's protection, Heph's skills for jewellery and trinkets, and Ares body for great sex. This was turning out to be a good day after all. She was really beginning to feel welcomed at Mount Olympus. She smiled, left the bed, and proceeded to wash down her body with water from a basin filled with cleansing lotions. She enjoyed his eyes feasting on her as she completed her bodily washing ritual. She picked up her previously discarded clothing and stepped into them.

'How will you explain your lengthy absence?' Ares was concerned.

'I'll tell them that I was so tired that I decided to have a rest,' she answered.

'That will work,' he agreed as he nodded.

She kissed him once more and then left him lying naked on her bed and she exited the room. She hastened down the long passageway back to the communal area. She was glad of the distance, as it gave her time to frame her mind into being back in the company of Athena, Zeus, Hera, and Hephaestus.

She stepped into the room. Selected a cup and poured herself some wine. She sat contentedly next to Heph who beamed with pleasure that she had chosen him to sit next to.

Zeus stood up and paced the room. He hurriedly refilled his cup and took a long drink from it. He then set the cup on the table, turned, and studied the others in the room. It was obvious that he had made up his mind about something. 'Aphrodite,' he began. 'I believe you need a husband. Being married will take the pressure off you from all the other men who will inevitably desire you. You are mesmerizingly beautiful, and many men will desire you.' He looked at Hera who gave him a quizzical look in return. It was obvious she was concerned with where he was going with this, and she now sat upright in her chair. Zeus felt secure enough to continue, 'Men will do stupid things for the favours of a woman, particularly one as desirable as you.'

Apparently, Hera agreed that her husband was right. He observed that she relaxed back into her chair.

As Zeus noticed the change in Hera's posture he decided to press on. 'I think our son would make a suitable husband for you.'

'Ares!?' Hera was aghast.

'No, not him!' Zeus contradicted. 'I meant this grinning idiot seated next to Aphrodite. I think she should marry Hephaestus,' Zeus concluded smiling broadly.

Athena shook her head in disbelief. She could not see this union working. Apparently, Hera shared her opinion. 'No!' Hera exclaimed. 'No, No, No! I absolutely forbid it. When you said our son, I believed you meant Ares and immediately I thought "Oh no, poor Aphrodite". The sex would be great but he is not the type of man any woman should marry. But for her to marry Hephaestus! No, absolutely not, I forbid it.'

Hephaestus reacted boldly to oppose his mother's forbiddance. 'But mother, I love her, and I believe she loves me!' He then reached over to hold Aphrodite's hand signalling their solidarity. She forced a smile and did not pull her hand away.

'I thought so,' Zeus grinned knowingly.

'Do you?' Hera challenged Aphrodite.

'When Heph proposed, I said I would consider it favourably. All these events are happening so fast, even by godly standards.'

'You proposed to her!?' Hera admonished her son.

'I love her,' Heph defended.

Athena now suppressed a chuckle. This situation was becoming more and more comical, but she did not want to insult her esteemed guests by laughing out loud.

'I think we should have a drink and congratulate the happy couple,' Zeus suggested and then refilled his cup, lift it in a salute, and drank the contents.

'Never! This must not happen. I will not allow it.' With that Hera raced across the room and grabbed Heph's hand and dragged him to the door. Heph reluctantly followed his mother, but he managed a brief wave goodbye to the woman he now loved so dearly. They left the room and exited Athena's home, with the door closing with a re-soundingly loud bang behind them.

Zeus looked at Aphrodite and Athena. 'She'll come around,' he reassured them.

'I think your wife doesn't like me at all,' Aphrodite concluded. She seems angry with me for some reason.

'You have only been here for five hours, and you have already managed to become the assassination target of an amorous monster. You've become engaged to one of our son's, and earlier on you have copulated twice with our youngest son.' He paused and smiled benevolently. 'You'll need to give Hera some time to warm up to you.'

Aphrodite initially looked perplexed, and then a little embarrassed. In a rare display, she blushed.

'We have an instinct for knowing that sort of thing,' Zeus explained.

'What should I do?' Aphrodite turned to Athena and Zeus for guidance.

'I think you should marry Hephaestus,' Zeus told her. 'It would be best that you were married so that you can stay here at Mount Olympus. If you do marry him, then Hera will eventually find it in herself to become accepting of you, especially if you give her grandchildren. Then you will be able to come and go as you please. If you do not, I fear that Hera will force you into exile.'

Aphrodite felt trapped and her face showed it.

'Go to bed and sleep on it,' Athena recommended to her.

'Alone,' Zeus cautioned.

***

From the waist up, Echidna was a stunningly beautiful woman, but from the waist down she had a snake's torso with an exceptionally long serpent's tail. She mostly lived in a cave far below the normal ground level. It was accessible to her by many long and narrow winding passageways that she alone knew how to navigate. It was her routine to slither up to the surface every morning and warm up her cold-blooded body. On a safe perch high near the cliffs edge, with the morning sun warming her from head to tail, she rested and felt good. Later in the morning, she would find a goat or two to snack on, and then she would return to her caves and slumber once more. Echidna was generally as content as any monster could be.

A loud unsettling noise startled her, and she quickly looked up, concerned that a giant eagle may foolishly try to claim her as a meal. Some had tried before, and although she did not really like eating these birds, she would do so when they inevitably failed in their attack when she smacked them down with her tail. Echidna did not like wasting food.

She finally found the source of the strange noise. A massive, multi-headed, multi-winged creature was heading directly toward her. Echidna was fascinated that something so big and ungainly could fly. As the hideous creature came nearer, she noticed coiled steel wrapped about its torso, hindering the creature's many arms. The beast landed with a resounding thump, close to where Echidna lay. Now curious, she slithered over to the creature that surprisingly became startled by her approach.

'Sorry,' She apologised. 'I didn't mean to scare you.'

'Oh,' the monster replied, uncertain if this creature was his potential enemy. His current predicament left him feeling somewhat vulnerable.

'Are you trapped?' Echidna asked mischievously.

Typhon was trapped, but he already knew how to release himself. He could shrink himself so small that the wire coil would no longer confine him. The problem was that by doing so, it would make him to the size of an easy meal for this half-woman half-snake creature that had just slithered up on him.

'I don't want you to eat me,' Typhon explained.

'You're too big for me!' Echidna laughed.

'In order to free myself, I will need to shrink myself and become small and become small enough so that these coils will then become loose. As I contract you may become tempted to devour me,' he explained.

'How small do you need to be?' she asked.

'About the size of a baby goat,' he replied.

'I understand your problem,' she replied winking at him. 'Baby goats happen to be my favourite meal.'

Both monsters remained quiet for a long time. They stared at the scenery, watched birds frolic, and occasionally they glanced at each other. Finally, it was Typhon who spoke. 'I would not actually become a goat.'

In a rare moment of hilarity, Echidna laughed loudly, and she enjoyed it. She leaned over to him and kissed him fully on the lips in appreciation.

Even though this surprised him, Typhon discovered that he also enjoyed the kiss, and even though he was still being held by the wire coil. He motioned to Echidna about some of the difficulty that he was experiencing.

'You poor thing, you do look decidedly uncomfortable,' she concluded.

Typhon nodded his agreement.

Echidna instantly decided that she really liked this male. Most she had met, quickly withdrew when they saw her with a snake's tail. This one was as ugly as you could get, but he seemed relaxed and comfortable with her appearance.

'Would you like me to turn away or are you okay shrinking with me watching you?' she asked with a mischievous smile.

'It is okay,' he assured her. He shrank his form until he was liberated from the wire grip, and he was soon able to step out from the coils. He smiled at her, bowed, and excused himself. 'I'll only be a moment,' he promised her.

Typhon stepped away from Echidna and grew to his full height. Numerous snake and dragon heads appeared from his neck and head. Hundreds of arms and hands grew from his torso. His multiple wings were now fully extended, and he roared a massive bellow in relief of being freed. The wind gust he projected flew from where he stood and hit a small fishing vessel that was well over the horizon. It pushed the tiny ship well off its course and doused the occupants with seawater. The worried fishermen were bewildered, but not injured. They tidied up the deck and resumed their work without ever understanding what had just happened to them.

Typhon then picked up and hurled the coiled wire into the ocean. It whizzed well over the fishermen's heads, startling them once more, before splashing noisily into the water.

When Typhon turned and re-joined Echidna, he saw that she had morphed into her human form. She was naked and he decided that he really liked what he saw. He quickly shrank back into his human form and sat naked beside her, sporting a mischievous grin.

'Feeling better?' she asked kindly.

'Much better, thank you,' he admitted. He then leaned forward, and they kissed some more. She moved her body so that she was now straddling his lap. Their embrace evolved and soon he was inside of her, each movement increasing the intensity of the pleasure of their copulation. They were vigorous and were able to climax many times before they finally separated in blissful exhaustion.

'Will you be staying long?' she asked, suddenly concerned that he soon would be leaving her.

'I would like to, if that is alright with you,' he replied politely. He decided that he liked Echidna a lot, and he felt safe and happy to be here with her.

'There are plenty of goats to eat.' She looked about as if looking for inspiration. 'Or if you prefer, you can eat fish.'

'Both will do nicely.' He smiled contentedly at her.

She relaxed happily into him. She was glad he came and hoped that he would remain with her for a long time.

Typhon spent his days between being with Echidna and wreaking havoc on pitiful mortals. He would summon up winds powerful enough to demolish their homes, and he would make their fishing fleets bounce dangerously on the enormous waves, sometimes even capsizing them. He became so well known for doing this, that they named these powerful windstorms after him.

In moments of tenderness, Typhon would wrap a loving arm around Echidna in a newfound lovers embrace. She smiled and laughed often, and they both realised that they were good together. He believed that he was happy as she was kind and loving toward him, and this was a first for him. He actually felt safe and content.

But he was just a tiny bit sad that she was not Aphrodite.

***

When Zeus returned home, he found his wife and their eldest son engaged in a verbal battle of wills. Ares was nowhere to be seen, presumably he was in his room sound asleep. Eileithyia and Hebe were both early to bed girls, but he was surprised that all the yelling between Hera and Heph had not arouse them and made them curious to learn why mother and son were arguing. Perhaps they knew better, and they purposefully stayed away in the safety and comfort of their own rooms. He smiled to himself.

'Why are you grinning?' Hera lashed out at him accusingly.

'You've always said that Heph should marry. Now that he has fallen in love and is ready to marry a beautiful woman, and now you are forbidding it,' Zeus explained trying hard not to sound too condescending.

'It is your fault that that woman is here. Why did you bring her to Mount Olympus?' Hera demanded avoiding Zeus's conclusion.

'It seemed the right thing to do at the time,' Zeus defended.

'All just so you could bed her!' Hera accused her husband's motives.

'No!' he lied.

'Mother!' Heph interjected. 'It's not just about having sex you know.'

Hera paused. It was true that for most males, it was just about the sex. But with Heph, perhaps there was something more. She folded her arms and looked at the two men suspiciously. She suddenly relaxed and smiled. 'I am going to bed,' she told them and turned and headed toward her sleeping chamber. She then stopped, turned, and looked at Zeus, smiling sweetly and then she murmured. 'Coming darling?'

Zeus knew that voice. He certainly did not need any convincing or require a second invitation.

***

The following morning, Hera awoke and stirred next to her husband. Their lovemaking was more vigorous than normal, and she felt better now that there was some release of her pent-up frustrations. They had obviously been building up deep within her. She looked out the window and it seemed that it was going to be another glorious sunny day at Mount Olympus. Her husband snored contentedly. She smiled and decided to let him sleep. He had earned it. She walked downstairs to see if any of the children were awake. She planned to have a quiet, calm conversation with Heph about his absurd plans of marrying Aphrodite. Perhaps he had already worked out the ridiculousness of his plan for himself. She had hoped so. She did not want to see her boy become emotionally devastated by this seductress.

When Hera stepped into the dining area, she was delighted to discover that a magnificent throne had recently been set up near the centre of the room. It was made of highly polished gold and silver. It caught the light from every direction, and it seemed to radiate magnificence. The craftsmanship was perfect and ornate, and she knew immediately that it could only have been crafted by Hephaestus. She walked up to it and stroked it with her fingertips, smudging it slightly. She immediately pulled down her sleeve and rebuffed the metal. She stepped back to admire it fully. It was brilliantly carved and assembled and decorated with multicoloured precious stones and metals that captured the morning sunlight and made it glow invitingly. The seat was soft and padded, as was the back rest. It looked solid, secure, and comfortable. She wondered how long her son had spent making it and why she had never known about its design and construction. The throne seat seemed to be too small for Zeus imposing bulk and so she concluded that the ceremonial chair was purposely built for her.

'Do you like it, mother?' Heph asked in a friendly voice.

'Oh Heph,' his mother's face expressed her praise for her son. 'I think it is the most beautiful thing you have ever made.'

'I made it especially for you mother,' Heph informed her.

'For me?' Hera feigned surprise.

'Yes mother. It was always going to be for you, but I finished it during the night so that I could present it to you this morning. I felt sad about what happened between us after we returned from Athena's home,' Heph explained.

'We did get a bit rowdy,' Hera conceded and nodded her agreement. She studied him and pushed out an endearing smile of reassurance.

'Would you like to try it?' Heph invited. He motioned for her to sit on the chair.

'May I?' Hera was being extra gentle and polite. She walked around the throne stroking it carefully, and smiled warmly at her son, appreciating his extraordinary efforts at reconciliation. She was being gracious about her son's thoughtful gift. She stepped up to the throne, turned and sat down. Instantly transparent clamps sprung from the chair's arms and legs, and another wrapped around her waist and held Hera tightly. She was uninjured but startled by the chairs designed entrapment. She struggled briefly, but the chair held her securely in place. Hera was now becoming enraged, and she summoned her godly abilities to release her, but her son's craftsmanship powers were too strong for her, and so she remained firmly trapped in place.

Hephaestus calmly walked up to his mother. To add insult to her predicament he planted a peck on her cheek. He stepped back and examined her. 'Are you comfortable, mother?' he asked casually, despite knowing that she was furious.

'Release me immediately!' she commanded.

He stepped nearer to his mother and in a composed and steady voice, he explained. 'When I believe that you sincerely approve of me marrying Aphrodite, and that you will be truly happy for us, then I will release you,' he told her with a half-smile. 'Right now, I am tired, and I need sleep.' Heph yawned, stretched, turned, and left his mother sitting on her prison throne hurling deafening, and exceptionally nasty expletives at her son's back.

***

While Heph slept, Hera had visitations from her husband and her two daughters. Ares was yet to make an appearance. He was not a morning person.

When Zeus discovered that his wife was being held captive by the chair he was immediately amused. He had to look closely at the transparent ties that bound her. Even from a short distance they were seemingly invisible. Ingenious he thought. He also correctly concluded that the workmanship was Heph's, and he assumed that her captivity was his way of countering his mother's negative feelings toward his intended. He neither smiled visibly, nor did he laugh out loud He even refrained from comment. He typically did what any husband would do under these unusual circumstances. He gave her a passionate kiss.

She did not reciprocate with any passion. When he withdrew, she admonished him. 'You could release me,' she demanded and began struggling futilely against the restraints.

'I could, but then I would have to permanently damage your beautiful chair and I wouldn't want to do that.' Zeus explained as he grabbed a wooden stool and placed it so he could sit before his wife. When it seemed to him that Hera had given up on the idea that she could struggle her way out of its hold, he continued. 'That would be a shame as it looks to be a magnificent chair, one that any parent would be proud off,' he added without smiling.

Hebe bounced happily into the room. She was a morning person and was delighted to see her mother in such a fine chair. She was also delighted to find her parents engaged in quiet conversation, as she thought they fought a little too often and both tended to use elevated voices to command the room. She fetched water in a cup for herself and then grabbed a stool so she could sit beside her father and in front of her mother.

'Wow mother. That is a fine-looking chair,' she complimented. 'Did Heph make it for you?'

'It is my prison.' she explained as she tried to pull her arms upward to demonstrate.

Hebe leaned forward and examined her mother's bounds. 'Oh yes, I see,' She confirmed. She sat down again and turned to her father to ask. 'Did Heph make this chair to punish mother?'

'Heph wants to marry Aphrodite, but your mother doesn't approve,' Zeus explained. Heph is making a point.

'It feels like coercion.'

'Oh.' Hebe stared at her mother. 'But you always said Heph should be married, and he would make some fortunate woman a fine husband.'

'Yes, but I obviously did not mean a woman like Aphrodite,' Hera retorted trying to remain calm.

'If Aphrodite wants to marry Heph, then it seems to me that we should be happy for him. As you know, he does not attract many candidates,' Hebe concluded solemnly.

'See,' Zeus agreed and smiled encouragingly at both women.

Next is was Eileithyia who entered the room. She was dressed as if about to go to work. She looked business like, as was her style when visiting the mortals who were about to give birth their baby. She spotted the three who were seated close together and decided to go to them to investigate. She then spotted her mother's restraints and was immediately concerned for her predicament.

'Did you do this to mother?' She asked her father accusingly.

'No.' he replied, unconcerned with the accusation.

'It was Heph that did it,' Hebe explained defending her father.

'Why would he do that?' Eileithyia demanded.

'He did it to encourage mother into agreeing to him about marry Aphrodite,' Hebe explained.

'Under duress.' Hera reiterated.

Eileithyia considered her mother's predicament and the situation with Heph. 'I think you should let him,' she told her mother and nodded knowingly.

'What! Why?' Hera was disappointed that even her favourite daughter had not taken her side.

'If it is what Heph and Aphrodite truly want, then why should anyone else care? Besides, Heph is a gullible man when it comes to women, and maybe marriage one will teach him some valuable lessons about us,' Eileithyia concluded. She turned and left the room and continued heading for a nearby village that had some pregnant mortals that were near to full term.

'See,' Zeus was pleased with the moral support he now felt from both his daughters.

So, it was in this way that Hera reluctantly changed her position and reluctantly agreed to Hephaestus' and Aphrodite's plans to marry.

***

Hera decided that the only way she could minimise the impact of their union was to take charge of everything. She was determined that the wedding was going to be a closed ceremony with only a few key immortals in attendance. As expected, Heph capitulated graciously when he learned of his mother's about face. He was delighted that his plan worked and was oblivious to the angst it had caused his mother. She was now agreeable and was even overseeing all the preparations to make his dream of marrying Aphrodite come true. Heph took this as a powerful endorsement and his two sisters who both knew better were kind enough not to shatter his delusion.

Aphrodite learned about her imminent nuptials from Athena. A messenger from Hera asked Athena to have Aphrodite prepared as a bride and brought to the palace to be formally wedded to Hephaestus. When Athena told her of what was happening, Aphrodite broke down and wept. She sobbed while Athena consoled her. In the end they concluded that the marriage was for the best. Heph was a kind man who would care for her and provide for her. It would allow her to stay in Mount Olympus and as she became better known by the other gods and goddess and her endearing personality charmed the humans, she would become quickly integrated into Mount Olympus society. Athena reminded Aphrodite that Zeus himself endorse their marriage and he was not the god to disagree with. Aphrodite eventually capitulated. She bathed, dressed in a simple and somewhat modest white dress that Athena organised for her. She then applied some facial moisturiser to hide the fact that she had been crying. Athena offered her some jewellery to wear but Aphrodite declined.

Athena escorted Aphrodite from her home to Zeus's palace, and she stood by her throughout the ceremony. Ares attended, but if he was concerned that Aphrodite was marrying his brother, he did not show it. Zeus officiated, and he said a few encouraging words before decreeing them wed. After the ceremony, Hera managed to give a welcoming peck on the cheek to her new daughter in-law. Hebe played hostess and served the wine. Eileithyia did not return in time from her duties and so did not attend. Some food and much wine were consumed, mostly by Ares, and Zeus, but the festivities were brief by Mount Olympus standards. Aphrodite was compliant and did all that she was beckoned to do. Only Heph grinned happily, but unfortunately for him, his happiness was to be short lived.

***

Aphrodite half-heartedly walked to her new home with her husband. She had had little time to come to terms with all the events that had taken place since her departure from Cyprus. She had only arrived at Mount Olympus a few days before, and now she was already married. It saddened her that she was maneuvered into marrying a man she did not love. She had bigger plans than just being his wife, and no quantity of gifts, jewellery, or trinkets, were ever going to change that. She liked him, and she initially enjoyed the fuss that he made over her. He was seemingly devoted to her happiness, and he was trying his best to please her, and make her happy. She laid back on their small bed, ready to consummate their union. He entered her, and after a few brief thrusts, his seed was suddenly spent inside her. She dutifully kissed him and thanked him, and he looked so happy and pleased with himself that she could almost forgive him.

After they had dressed, she looked about the room becoming curious about her new home. Much of it looked, felt, and smelt like a workshop. Heph immediately sensed her disdain. 'I'll clean it up for you,' he promised. 'I'll keep one part of our home free from my tools and projects, so that we can make it our happy place,' he assured her, grinning happily.

Aphrodite managed a smile and then became curious. 'Tell me about your leg.' It was rare for an immortal to be permanently damaged.

'When I was still a little boy, I walked into my mother's bed chamber. I had had a bad dream and I wanted her to comfort me,' he replied remembering. 'My father was in a terrible mood. My mother had just accused him of being with another woman. I did not understand what was happening at the time, as I was too little. I believed he was going to hit her, and so I ran to protect her just as father wielded his fist. I was thrown against the wall and my leg broke. My mother sent me to Lemnos to have my leg mended and for my protection. Lemnos was a place that had many skilled physicians that worked and resided there. As skilled as they were they could heal the wound but not prevent the limp. The damage caused by my angry father was permanent. If it had been inflicted by any other god, other than the king of the gods himself, they assured me that I would have fully recovered.'

Aphrodite suddenly felt sorrowful for her poor husband. She reached out to him to give him a comforting hug and he appreciated her gesture by snuggling up close to her. She held him briefly, and then asked. 'Does your father often beat your mother?'

'No, never. I was mistaken. He never has hit her or any of his children. I just got in the way of his fist. I guess that makes my injury mostly my own fault.'

'When did you return to Mount Olympus?' she asked kindly.

'Not until I was fully grown-up. The people of Lemnos were wonderful to me. They did their best to heal my leg, and they were gentle and loving toward me. They taught me my skills as a blacksmith and jeweller. I still visit them regularly as we are still very close. Now, I am their protector,' he explained smiling at the memory of living with them. He turned lovingly toward Aphrodite and continued. 'When I returned to Mount Olympus, I showed my father my skills and he was impressed. I make powerful lightning bolts for him, and I know that I have earned his respect. We have gotten along just fine in all the time since my return,' he assured her. 'I also know that it was father who encouraged my mother to allow us to be married.'

Aphrodite looked away feeling depressed. For some reason, she did not want her new husband to see her face displaying her unhappiness.

***

Over the next few months, Aphrodite tried her best to settle into married life. Heph was happily making all manner of jewellery and trinkets to please her. Their lovemaking's was infrequent and brief, and no progeny emerged from their union. Heph was unperturbed. He was kept busy supervising the construction and repairs of the numerous palaces and houses that were required by the gods and their attendants. He supervised the expansion of his own workshop and had many workers that were required smithing and repairing the objects, both useful and ornamental, to all the other gods and goddesses of Mount Olympus. The love Heph felt from being married to Aphrodite energized him.

Stories of Aphrodite's beauty and attractiveness quickly spread across the Greek world. She no longer felt sexy and now habitually remained clothed. Despite her newfound modesty, and her lack of actual sexual experience, she somehow became known as the Goddess of love, lust, romance, and passion. The workshop was as busy as ever with curiosity seekers commissioning work from Hephaestus just in order to catch a glimpse of her.

Aphrodite did her best to turn their living quarters in their part of the workshop, into a liveable home. She also supervised her attendants who worked tirelessly to please her. They were all half-sisters of Heph, and they were delighted to serve her. Their mother, Eurynome chose never to live at Mount Olympus, as she was permanently afraid of Hera's retribution for having once been Zeus's lover. It was also because she preferred her natural form over her human form. Eurynome was bottom half fish and top half a magnificent woman. She preferred to live in the ocean. Her daughters wanted to make other plans, and when they learned they could be at Mount Olympus, they leapt with joy at the opportunity to serve the goddess of love, beauty, lust, and desire. They all wanted some loving and desiring for themselves, and they correctly calculated that working for Aphrodite was the right place to live to get some.

Aglaia quickly became known as the goddess of grace, splendour, and beauty. Whilst she was no match for Aphrodite, she was a magnificently beautiful woman in her own right. She posed no threat to Aphrodite's title as the most beautiful or most desirable woman, and she ensured that everyone saw her as being in a subservient role to her mistress. As it turned out, Aphrodite was actually appreciative that Aglaia was able to distract some of the many suitors that would have otherwise pestered her.

Thalia became known as the goddess of grace of good cheer. She was naturally very personable. Her feet seemed to barely touch the ground whenever she walked, or danced, to wherever she was doing. She was also radiantly beautiful and seemed to be always in a positive mood. She was ever attendant as it pleased her to please, and she was a delight to all who met her. She was exceptionally resourceful in organising food for banquets at short notice. She had her fair share of male admirers, but she always managed to remain discreet about any liaisons she experienced. Aphrodite often vocalised her praise for Thalia and her appreciation of her organisational skills.

Euphrosyne was soon known as the goddess for grace, merriment, and charm. She was and enormous help at pacifying disgruntled visitors to Hephaestus' workshop, as well as resolving any tension or disputes that infrequently occurred between the women. She was also a beautiful woman and Hephaestus considered himself fortunate to be surrounded by them. Aphrodite considered herself fortunate to be attended by them, and she secretly hoped that one day her husband would succumb to the temptation and bed one of them, or all of them, she did not care which. She was reluctant to take a lover as she feared Hera's wrath. She concluded that if Heph would be the first to do so it would make it all right for her, but it now seemed that it might never happen.

The numbers of Aphrodite's followers and worshipers continued to grow, and so they were appreciative to have such a dedicated team to control the flow of visitors. Trade boomed as a result, with many financial offerings being made in exchange for trinkets featuring Aphrodite's image. Hephaestus cleverly designed them to last for only a short time, which enhanced their demand.

The three Graces fussed over Hephaestus as equally as they served Aphrodite. She therefore had very few opportunities to rendezvous with the god she felt would become her true lover, Ares.

Aphrodite kept her melancholy in check and for now she remained faithful to her marriage.

***

Far away from Mount Olympus, Typhon gently wrapped a blanket around Echidna's shoulders. The night air was cooling as winter was approaching. Being cold blooded Echidna was susceptible to the cold and he was caring enough to want to comfort her. The two had become very close during his time with her.

'Do you ever hibernate?' Typhon was curious.

'Would you miss me if I did?' Echidna replied.

'Yes.'

'I can hibernate if I choose to. But I only do so when I am bored or if the food supply is short. With you, I am never bored.'

They examined each other's faces, smiled, and then kissed.

***

Aphrodite's now famed beauty and her legendary power over love and desire became so well known to all the gods and mortals alike that she became the most talked about resident of Mount Olympus. Being the daughter in law of Zeus and Hera added to her reputation, as did being married to such a skilled craftsman. As unhappy as she was at being married to Heph, she did enjoy the admiring attentions of all who came to meet her. She thought it ironic that her reputation far exceeded her actual lifestyle, and it made her sad that she was missing out on so much in order to be faithful to a man who could not truly appreciate her sexuality.

Their lovemaking had improved only a little, despite her patient attempts to steer him into a greater understanding of the pleasures of woman. He seemed happy to be with her, but he remained distracted with all the projects in the workshop.

One day, during a festival in her honour, a lonely king from Cyprus named Pygmalion sought out Aphrodite at her husband's workshop. He had fallen hopelessly in love with an ivory statue of a gorgeous woman that he had carved. He begged Aphrodite, 'Ye Gods, who can do all things, I pray you give me a real wife just like my wife of ivory.' He showed Aphrodite the statue and she could sense his commitment and true love for his figurine. She was so moved by his love for her, that she caused the flame on her altar to shoot up from three places to form into a fiery point. She then spoke to Pygmalion and told him. 'Go home and rejoice and be in love.'

When Pygmalion returned home, he laid the statue carefully on a pillow in his bed. The following morning, he awoke to discover that his ivory wife was now a real human woman. He named her Galatea after her milky-white complexion. They remained together and they were in love and happy. She soon bore him and healthy, loving, and congenial baby daughter that they named Paphos.

***

Sadly, for Aphrodite, the sexual encounters between her and her husband remained infrequent and boringly predictable. Whilst he was overjoyed with their arrangement, she was not. However, one day Aphrodite approached her husband with some news. Her tummy now showed, and she could no longer withhold the announcement. She was with child. Heph was ecstatic and he quickly arranged a party to celebrate the joyous news. Everyone who was anyone came to help them celebrate.

Aglaia was busy coordinating the guests. Thalia was engaged organising food and drinks. Euphrosyne arranged the entertainment. Everyone was busy and everyone but Aphrodite, was overjoyed with the news.

Dionysus, the God of wine and altered states was an adopted son of Zeus, and as a favoured friend to both Zeus and Athena, he granted them some immunity over his influences. This did not extend to Zeus's sons however, and during the night of celebrating the news of their first impending child, Dionysus got Hephaestus helplessly drunk, and he then stripped him naked, painted him with red wine, and sat him on a mule. Dionysus next led him through the passageways of Mount Olympus in a parade before the other gods and goddesses who howled with laughter. Even Hera was able to see the fun of it, but later she took pity on him and helped clean him up. As a result, they became reconciled and were close once more.

Soon Aphrodite gave birth to a handsome baby boy. Aphrodite chose to name their son, Eros. Heph was overjoyed and spruiked his plans for him and his son, to his parents, and sisters who had come to visit and welcome the new family member into their world. Heph's happiness was shattered when Hera examined the baby. 'He does look a lot like Ares,' she said plainly.

When Heph could see for himself that it was true, and the guilty expression on Aphrodite's face confirmed it, Heph immediately left Mount Olympus and journeyed to Lemnos to gather his thoughts and spend time with his trusted friends.

***

Eros grew rapidly. He had his mother's natural beauty, and he quickly became known as the god of desire. He could grow wings when he wanted them, and he would often fly. He carried a lyre and a flute which he played melodiously, and he was always armed with a bow and an endless supply of customised arrows that were so small that they inflicted no injury and were perfectly designed to deliver his potions. His mother adored him, and they were almost inseparable. Aphrodite, now free of her husband's hindrance, spent most of her time with Ares. Their affair was now publicly known, and apart from Hera and Athena, no-one cared.

Eros remained slight of build, which helped him hover when flying above anyone that interested him. He delighted in bequeathing love and desire on any mortals that he approved of. He also enjoyed taking it away from them. If he did not like the couple he observed, or if they were unkind to him in some way, he would shoot one arrow laced with potion into one of them, rendering them hopelessly in love, and shoot a different potion into the other, filling them with disdain. It is because of Eros, that love and relationships have remained thoroughly unpredictable throughout eternity.

Eros's small frame and childlike behaviour became an increasingly concern for Aphrodite. Themis advised her to have another child, a brother, as this would make Eros bulk up as he would have the responsibility for a younger sibling. Aphrodite agreed and she rendezvoused once more with an enthusiastic Ares, and soon after, Anteros was born. True to Themis's promise, her older son quickly filled out and significantly physically matured. Anteros also grew rapidly into adulthood, and he became the god of true love, and the avenger of unrequited love. He too was winged, and he also carried a bow and many arrows.

Both of Aphrodite's sons had quickly grown up to be athletic, muscular, and strikingly handsome. They looked so similar to each other that even Aphrodite was sometimes confused as to who was who. To help her, Eros decided to keep his hair length short, while Anteros agreed to keep his hair long, a decision which was much to their mother's relief. Eros also enjoyed his sexual escapades with other men and proudly became known as the protector of true love between men. However, his brother Anteros only ever enjoyed sexual activities with willing beautiful women. This arrangement worked well, and they never once competed for a lover. They both loved to surprise a stranger with the gift of a single magnificent rose, and then assign the bequest to a total stranger, just to watch what resulted between them. The brothers were great friends, mutual pranksters, and sometimes they could be seen naked when accompanying their equally naked mother walking through the markets and streets of Mount Olympus, just to see if they could titillate observers.

***

Helios, God of the sun, decided to visit Hephaestus while he was living at Lemnos. Helios was troubled by Aphrodite's highly visible affair with Ares and was worried that Aphrodite's behaviour would be mimicked by other goddesses and by human females. He felt that Aphrodite was personifying debauchery, and so he advised Heph to intercede and to make them end it before it was too late. Reluctantly and with much trepidation, Heph returned home to Mount Olympus to deal with his unfaithful wife. He was relieved to find that in his absence his workshop was being properly managed by the Three Graces. His workers toiled productively, patrons were satisfied, and his property and possessions were well maintained and kept secure. The three women were pleased to see him and wanted to know all about where he had been, but they were reluctant to discuss their mistress's activities.

Heph instinctively knew that he would find her at Ares's palace. He grabbed a bag and marched toward Ares's home with purpose, intending to catch them in the act of infidelity. He quietly entered the palace and walked softly into Ares's bed chamber. There he found them in the throes of sweaty adultery. He reached into his bag and flung a magnificent net that was as fine as gossamer and as strong as adamantine. It landed over the two of them, instantly fusing the two of them together and capturing them in the act of copulation. Heph ran from the building shouting to everyone that they should come to witness their betrayal. Many entered the chamber to see them, but they just howled with laughter at Aphrodite's and Ares's predicament. Sadly, no-one sympathised with poor Hephaestus. Their adultery was old news, and no one cared. Finally, Heph released his wife and brother. Ares had to promise to pay some gold in compensation to his older brother, but later he claimed it was worth it just to have regular great sex, without all the complicated commitments, with someone who was as fantastic as Aphrodite.

Heph was crestfallen when he returned to his workshop. He did not see Aphrodite or Ares for some time. He eventually got back to his work, and he remained bitter about them for the rest of his immortal life.

***

The women of Lemnos had felt so indignant about Aphrodite's cruel treatment of Hephaestus that they permanently withdrew their homage of her. Aphrodite learned of their actions and in her revenge, and without Hephaestus' knowledge, she burdened all the woman on the island with a noxious body odour that repulsed their husbands and any potential suitors. No amount of body washing, or mouth sprays, could remove the offensive smell. When Heph learned of their predicament he was furious at their treatment, but he was powerless to intercede. The men of Lemnos met to discuss the problem. Collectively, they resolved that they deserved love and the comfort of loving good smelling women. At a meeting they agreed to entice pleasant smelling woman from Thrace to marry them and to have their children with them.

The women of Lemnos learned of these plans and became furious and turned hostile toward their islander men. They gathered knives, hunted them down and slaughtered all of them. The only exception was their King, whose name was Thoas, who they permanently exiled. When the Thracian woman arrived by boat the sailors saw the Lemnos women's rage they turned and fled. For a brief period, the island was only populated with Lemnos women. Over time, their body odour problem dissipated, and the women were lonely and aggrieved. One day, sailors from the sailing ship The Argo, briefly visited to their island. The Argo's captain was named Jason and his quest meant that their stay was brief, but by the time they departed, he and his sailors left behind an island populated with many pregnant women.

***

At Mount Olympus, Ares arranged a separate palace for Aphrodite to live in with her two sons. Aglaia, Thalia, and Euphrosyne, also moved in with her. For the most they were happy and carefree. Euphrosyne soon developed a casual sexual relationship with Anteros, and Aphrodite seemed pleased to see them happily enjoying each other's company and bodies.

Aglaia, Thalia, and Euphrosyne continued to visit Hephaestus and they often stayed with him when Aphrodite journeyed away from Mount Olympus. He doted on them in a paternal way which the women really enjoyed.

Aphrodite spent much of her time copulating with Ares at his palace and this often resulted in more offspring. They named a baby boy, Deimos, who became the god of terror and another child, also a male, Phobos, and he grew up to become the god of fear. Deimos and Phobos grew quickly into adulthood. Soon, Eris, the goddess of strife and discord, and Enyo, goddess of war, bloodshed, and violence, became enamoured with them, and so they moved in with them also. All four readily accompanied Ares into his battles, and he came to love and respect all of them for their fierceness, cunning, and strategic planning skills. They readily aided him when preparing for battle and joined him in carrying out violent acts during their numerous campaigns and invasions with the human warriors.

Ares's palace became well known as a place used for lustful practices and the pursuit of physical pleasures. Many humans sought out and some gained invitations into the palace. These mortals readily surrendered themselves to be at the pleasure of the gods and goddesses. They were mostly used for copulation and then were often casually discarded. Some of the good-looking humans were initially ordered to disrobe and pose as naked living statues, and then later as a reward they were allowed to join in the fun. Those humans that showed any reluctance to participate were sent to the kitchens to prepare and serve food, or they were ordered to pour wine. Other humans who were intimidated by the activities were bullied and ridiculed and they were tasked with cleaning up the palace as most of the activities within Ares's chambers were both messy and smelly. Only a few humans were actually harmed during their participation, and all of them left the palace with fantastic stories to tell, which further enhanced human interest into arranging a visit to Ares's palace.

Dionysus, the God of wine and altered states was a frequent and welcomed guest at Ares palace, but secretly he reported on their continuing misdeeds and robust sexual adventures to Zeus. Instead of being angry, Zeus was actually entertained by these accounts, and he welcomed Dionysus's reports of his youngest son's proclivities.

***

Adonis was regarded by many of the Greek goddesses as being the most handsome and beautiful human male that they had ever seen. He was born from a consenting incestuous relationship that his mother Myrrah had had with her father, Theias. Both Aphrodite and Hades wife, Persephone became enamoured with him, and they both equally desired to pamper him and bed him. Their competitiveness quickly became a problem and the two women publicly brawled over who would have him. So, Zeus decreed that Adonis would spend one third of his time with Aphrodite and one third of his time with Persepone and the remaining third of his time with whomever he chose.

Sadly, Adonis's time with both Aphrodite and Persephone ended tragically when he died from his wounds after being gored by a massive wild boar on a hunting trip. Aphrodite symbolised his death by manifesting Anemone flowers from his spilt blood. She also arranged an annual midsummer festival to mourn his death.

***

One day, Aphrodite learned about a beautiful woman named Psyche. She was the daughter of a king. She was so beautiful and charming that many men were captivated by her elegance that they came to desire her more than they did Aphrodite. Numerous men, both single and married, travelled great distances just to meet with her, and perhaps to win her favours. As the interest level in Aphrodite fell dramatically, she became intensely jealous of Psyche and publicly declared. "Am I then to be eclipsed in my honours by a mortal girl? But she will not go on so quietly to usurp my honours. I will give her cause to repent of so unlawful a beauty!"

She summoned Eros and ordered him to perform an important task. 'My dear son, punish that contumacious beauty; give your mother a revenge as sweet as her injuries are great; infuse into the bosom of that haughty girl a passion for some low, mean, unworthy being, so that she may reap a mortification as great as her present exultation and triumph.'

So, Eros travelled to the kingdom, and he found the beautiful Psyche asleep in her bed chambers. He had previously filled two amber vases with water from each of the two fountains in Aphrodite's Garden. He then prepared two arrows. One he dipped in sweet water, the other in the bitter. He tipped bitter water from the vase over her lips to complete his mother's instruction. She awoke in utter panic, and this so startled Eros that he inadvertently stabbed himself with his own arrow, the one laced with sweet water. This immediately caused him to feel lovingly toward Psyche, and he now desperately wanted to reverse the effects of the bitter water he had already applied to her. He gave her the sweet water to drink to neutralise its power.

As Eros's wound quickly healed and the powers inserted by the arrow soon wore off. However, Psyche was a mortal and so she remained deeply in love with Eros. But sadly, for her, Eros now rejected her. He told her that as a mortal she was now forbidden to look at him. Eros was tired from his journey, and he located a sleeping chamber to rest before he returned home. But Psyche was now so deeply in love with Eros that she felt compelled to disobey him. Above all other considerations she had to be with Eros. She snuck into the darkened room where he slept and lit a lamp so that she could gaze lovingly at him. Hot oil from the lamp dripped onto Eros's shoulder, burning him. He was so angry that she had burnt him and disobeyed him by coming to see him that he cast a curse on her. From now on, no mortal would ever love her. He then abandoned her into her father's care and hastily returned alone to Mount Olympus to report his success to his mother. He explained to Aphrodite that the deed was done, and then he proceeded to forestalled her from asking for further details by telling her of a drink he had just created in her honour. He called it "The Aphrodisiac," as it encourages the drinker into unrestrained exuberance, love, and lust. He showed her the remains of the sweet water from the amber vase. She was most pleased with his thoughtfulness, and she hugged him in gratitude.

Sadly, Psyche remained alone for many years. Men continued to acknowledge her beauty, but none wanted her as a wife. Her two sisters were now long married, and she grew older alone. She eventually sought out an oracle who told her that for her, true love only existed at Mount Olympus. She was told that she must drink the water from Aphrodite's fountain to break the curse. She packed lightly and soon embarked on the journey to Mount Olympus. On her arrival she joined a procession of worshippers and entered the temple of Aphrodite. She was able to sneak past the guards and succeeded in drinking directly from the fountain of sweet water and she was instantly rejuvenated. When Aphrodite saw her, she challenged her presence in her home. After a lengthy discussion, Aphrodite eventually understood and forgave her intrusion on condition she pay penance by completing many tasks and rituals that Aphrodite assigned her. Psyche was eventually accepted and forgiven for her beauty. Eros was soon aware of Psyche's arrival and the terms of her punishment. He felt truly guilty for his earlier treatment of her, and he also realised that he still had feelings of love for her. They became so compelling that he could no longer dismiss them. He decided to declare his love for Psyche to Aphrodite who petitioned Zeus, who met her and had looked favourably upon Psyche. She was allowed to remain at Mount Olympus as an immortal. Eros and Psyche soon had a daughter they named, Pleasure. Psyche later became known as the goddess of the personification of the human soul.

***

Sadly for Typhon, he could not get Aphrodite out of his thoughts and desires. Echidna was always there for him, and together they produced many monstrous off-springs which they delighted in placing in various locations throughout the Greek lands, with instructions on how to have fun and harm all humans. However, as much he loved Echidna, Typhon remained enamoured by Aphrodite's charms and beauty. He eventually decided to visit Mount Olympus and try one more time to consummate his lust for this ultimate of all women.

He bid Echidna goodbye without explanation. If she knew or felt any anguish over his lust for the other woman, she never showed it. They kissed and he departed. His journey was uneventful. He had spotted an opportunity to blow a strong wind and torment human's and their endeavours, which did not require much effort on his part, but was distracted with thoughts of passion. Typhon was preoccupied dreaming with high hopes of Aphrodite willingly returning his love and affections.

Typhon landed unobserved next to a stream that was both downhill and downwind from Mount Olympus. He changed into his human form, stripped, and bathed in a stream. When he was dry, he began anointing himself with lotions that he had arranged after learning about their pleasing properties with women. He had not risked testing them on Echidna as he knew that she would not like them. But he felt confident that they would enhance his chances with the goddess of love and beauty. He dressed into clothing that was made from red silk that felt good against his skin. He felt wonderful and he smiled at his reflection in the pond as he busily used the water to tidy his hair.

His walk to the many palaces, alters, shops, and houses that made up the gods capital was also pleasant. The road was well maintained and seemingly popular. There were many humans, workers, worshippers, and tourists alike that made the journey into Mount Olympus, and he felt confident that he fitted in perfectly. Typhon overheard an excited group of male travellers who talked about their planned visit to the shrine of Aphrodite, and their anticipation of actually meeting her. He smiled congenially at them and decided to tag along and merge with their party. They didn't seem to care about him, and he felt confident that he blended in. Soon they approached the shrine erected for Aphrodite worshipers. There was a queue which they happily joined. He was supporting his carefree smile when he spied Athena. At first, he hesitated but then decided that she would not recognise him in his fine red clothing and his pleasantly scented body lotions. He broke from the queue and cautiously approached Athena.

'Forgive my boldness,' he said as he approached her and bowed.

Athena was one of the more accessible goddesses of Mount Olympus. She often gave impromptu counsel to mortals who needed immortal assistance. 'How may I help you?' she was amused by his bright red attire. She had recognised Typhon immediately, but she could tell that while he was in this disguise, and by his manner, that he was in no hurry to make any mischief.

'I seek an audience with Aphrodite,' he confessed. 'Are you by any chance, friends with her?'

Once, when Aphrodite had first arrived at Mount Olympus, Athena had tried to become friends with Aphrodite but that had long ago dissipated. Whilst she disapproved of her promiscuous behaviour, her general lack of attire, and her unproductive outlook on life, she had generally maintained her own counsel. 'I am acquainted with Aphrodite,' she answered politely.

Typhon continued smiling, but now his eyes smiled also. 'Would you know her relationship status?' he asked cautiously.

'She became married to Hephaestus,' Athena told him.

Typhon's face fell.

'But their marriage didn't work,' She continued.

The smile returned.

'So, she is now partnered with Ares,' she added.

The smile vanished.

'But theirs is an open relationship.'

The smile returned.

Athena studied his face. Typhon was obviously still infatuated with Aphrodite. She decided that in the interests in peace and harmony at Mount Olympus that it would be better if this monster, despite the impressive effort he was making, dismiss his plans for pursuing his romantic infatuation of Aphrodite. She sternly added, 'They do have many children together and she seems happy being committed to him,' Athena concluded pressing these facts onto Typhon.

The smile vanished once more. 'I see.' Typhon replied, the sadness resonated in his voice. He felt devastated and his body language confirmed it.

'Truly, she isn't worthy of your love or respect,' Athena tried to sound kindly. 'Aphrodite has a wicked streak, and you should be wary of falling in love with her. Don't you have someone special in your life?' she asked hopefully. Athena already knew about his relationship with Echidna and had dealt firsthand with their monstrous offspring.

Typhon thought immediately of Echidna. 'I do,' he conceded. He then smiled at the thought of her loving patience with him. He realised that he did love her, but he also knew that it was a different kind of love that he felt about Aphrodite.

'Return home to your true love, and forget Aphrodite,' Athena advised.

'I will,' Typhon nodded his capitulation.

Athena was much relieved to hear this news.

Typhon turned and walked away. He felt dejected and hurt. In his mind, he and Aphrodite would become the ultimate of all lovers, and they would be the envy of all others. He left Mount Olympus feeling sad and sorrowful, he discarded his red silk clothing, formed his wings, rose, and set off home to Echidna. But suddenly, his grief soon turned to anger, and he whisked up a powerful windstorm that destroyed many homes, sank numerous vessels, killed many people, and drowned much livestock. If he had realised the extent of the devastation that he had just caused, he did not show it and he certainly would not care.

***

For a brief time, Aphrodite was tasked with indoctrinating and socialising a beautiful young woman named Pandora. She was commissioned by Zeus and hand crafted by Hephaestus to be the role model for all human women. She delighted teaching Pandora all the bad things about men and how to dominate them in relationships. Pandora somehow survived the experience, and she eventually married Prometheus's brother Epimethius. Together they lived a quiet peaceful life, helping women wherever they can.

***

There was an interesting young woman who was named Atalanta. It was said that she had a face that was too boyish for a girl, yet too girlish to be a boy. Yet, many men thought her highly desirable. She attempted to dissuade her many suitors by dressing herself in men's clothing. Many believed that under all those garments there was a body that rivalled Aphrodite herself. This was even though she only bathed privately and was generally exceptionally modest. Yet despite her public vows of celibecy, her reputation grew, and she was forever plagued by mostly male suitors who believed they could woo her into a physical loving relationship.

Atalanta preferred doing manly activities as opposed to those that were traditionally reserved for females. She was a close friend of Artemis, and she would often join her in a hunt. Artemis was respected for her skills with bow and arrows and with spears. Atalanta was also a swift runner and could match Artemis in both speed and manoeuvrability when they ran through the woods and forests together. She was also very capable with bow and arrows but wise enough not to be better than Artemis.

It was as a young woman that she was advised to never fall in love. She was told that all men would seek to take away her free-spirited ways with unreasonable demands. They would have excessive rules and restrictions that would constantly sadden her. She was also told that she could never be happy being married to any man, as they would inevitably try to dominate her. She had come close to falling in love only once during a massive boar hunt. He was a prince of Calydonia whose name was Meleager, but he died mysteriously before their romance could ever blossom.

So, she now devoted herself to running and the thrill of the chase during the hunt. Her open vow of spinsterhood only made her more attractive to suitors, and there were many. Their numbers swelled, and they were persistent, and were now becoming increasingly bothersome. So, Atalanta contrived a new plan to permanently dissuade them, and she publicly made her announcement. 'If any man can prove his worthiness by besting me in a running race, then I'll happily submit to marrying him,' Atalanta explained to the group of eager men.

Over the days that followed the interest in her now rose dramatically, so she decided to add the following deterring caveat. 'But any man that loses the race, and is outrun by me, will at once submit themselves for execution.' Atalanta was certain that this would dissuade all those men and that they would hastily depart and permanently leave her alone.

Now, if Atalanta would have consulted her wise elders, they would have explained to her some things about the male ego. Any man who thought himself to be brave and mighty could not possibly withdraw from such a challenge. They feared looking weak more than they feared for their lives. He would run in order to prove that he was man enough to achieve victory, win the challenge, and earn her hand in marriage. Her clever plan for a solitary life backfired, and she was now more popular than ever.

The running races were organised, and several executioners were recruited. Atalanta ensured that they were positioned in full view of the participants and were close to the finish line. Their razor-sharp polished swords glistened in the sunlight, and the executioners delighted their audience by twirling them theatrically through the air, and then carving up mounted melons with a display of skills. Yet, none of the runners were dissuaded from racing. They all believed that they could best any female and that the only real challenge they faced was to beat the other male runners and be first over the line.

Prince Hippomenes was asked to witness and judge the fairness of each race. When he learned the planned fate of the losers, he was shocked, and so he confronted Atalanta. 'Please, Atalanta. These conditions you have set are monstrous. I ask you to withdraw them as I fear many good men will die to prove their worthiness,' Hippomenes pleaded.

'I cannot,' she replied. 'If I do not do this now, then men will always pursue me. I must maintain my resolve, and once and for all deter this persistent and annoying male interest in me. Besides, when the first group of runners are dispatched by the executioners, the rest will withdraw.'

'Do you prefer the company of a woman?'

'No, not in that way. I only want one man in my life, and I have yet to meet him. It is the relentless multitude that I must now forever discourage. Their persistence constantly stresses me.'

'Are you very fast?' he asked unsure of her ability.

'I am the fastest, I run with Artemis,' she replied, and he understood her meaning. 'I guarantee you that I will win every race.' Her face was stoic.

Hippomenes now believed that it was Artemis that was behind her plan. She was also an exceptional runner, and she had also sworn to remain a virgin. Her influence on this event was very apparent, and now Hippomenes feared that Atalanta would win each race and that all these suitors would be put to death. He approached the group of men. 'Hear me,' he pleaded, attracting their immediate interest as he would be determining the fairness of their races. 'Atalanta runs with Artemis, and I know that she cannot be beaten,' he warned them.

Only a few men were dissuaded and turned to leave. Most stayed, grinning like idiots, flexing, and stretching their muscles. There were so many men, and it was impractical to run each race individually. Hippomenes decided that groups of five men would race Atalanta in each event. In this way it would only take six races to get through this group of suitors. He now hoped that many of the men would withdraw when they witnessed the execution of the losers at the end of the first race.

When Atalanta saw the look of distress on Hippomenes face, and she instantly felt sorry for him. 'I can see that you are unhappy,' she told him when they were in close proximity.

'These idiots will die trying to win you as their bride, when they should be trying to marry someone who loves and respects them. They must know that you do not love any of them, so I do not understand what they are hoping to achieve. Besting you is only a short-term victory, especially if you do not grow to love the winner after you are married.

'How could I love ever him, or respect him, when I know what he is willing risk just to win?' Atalanta confronted. 'This race will only prove their running speed. It will never prove their suitability to be my husband. I planned this to dissuade suitors, not to find a husband.'

Hippomenes sighed. He was touched by her dilemma, and it showed on his face. Atalanta gave him a comforting smile. She reached up and touched his face. 'Maybe you should run against me, you are a kind man and very thoughtful and respectful. I might even let you win,' she teased.

Some men were eager to be in the first group of five to run. They wanted to win her and so they had to be in the first group to ensure they were in a better position to do so. If she lost to a man in the first race the other races would be cancelled. Some others wanted to be in the last race, as they were hoping that Atalanta would be tired and, therefore she would be easier to beat. Hippomenes decided to draw names from a bucket and in this way the first five men were chosen. Atalanta and the first five men moved to the start line. She surprised them all by disrobing, preferring to run naked. There were numerous gasps from the runners and the people in the crowd. Atalanta's body was lithe and muscular, but somehow also slender. She was perfection and Hippomenes now found that he himself was also captivated by her beauty.

The rules were simple. Run when told to do so, and the first man to finish ahead of Atalanta would win her in marriage. He shouted 'run!' The six runners ran as swiftly as they could, but Atalanta was too fast for all of them. At the finish line the five exhausted men were swiftly dispatched, too tired to offer any resistance. Atalanta did not watch as she had already turned away and sprinted back to the starting line, ready to run her next race. At this point, some of the men decided to withdraw from the competition. They saw how fast she really was, and they were horrified by the swift death of the losing males. But, despite the carnage, it still took another two more races to end the event. Each group of losing men met the same fate as the first five. The butchery was terrible, and their bodies were haphazardly stacked high on a cart to be taken away for a simple and quick burial.

Atalanta was ashen faced as she felt much distress over their deaths.

When Atalanta was clothed once more, Hippomenes gave her a beverage and some comfort. They talked at length about the races and how badly she felt for the men's families. They would be grieving, and she decided that she would never use this method to discourage men ever again. Hippomenes soon felt an awareness that he had not felt for any woman before. He realised that he too had fallen under her spell, and that now he too desired her. He had met many eligible women, and he was encourage to marry but had not yest met the right woman. He started to feel that this had to be true for her also, so he decided to declare himself. 'I find myself having strong feelings of affection for you, Atalanta,' he explained to her.

'I can sense it also,' she agreed.

'May I woo you?' he asked.

Atalanta looked about the crowds who had remained in the expectation that more was about to happen.

'Under these circumstances, you would have to beat me in a running race.'

'Would you let me win?'

She smiled. 'I will try,' she promised. 'I have just run three races, and the crowd may believe that I am tired and raced out.'

Hippomenes started his preparations for the race. In his tent he prayed to an image of Aphrodite asking her to give him increased speed as he ran for true love. Now, unknown to Hippomenes, Aphrodite and her son Eros were among the crowd, and they had witnessed the events. Aphrodite was close by and had heard his prayer to her and took kindness toward him.

To Hippomenes surprise, his favoured goddess entered his tent and approached him. 'Hippomenes, you are deeply in love, and I sense that Atalanta is in love with you also,' Aphrodite spoke gently summarising the situation. 'I will help you win your race, and her heart, and I will ensure that the two of you will become happily married.'

'Thank you,' Hippomenes cried and was overjoyed. Without being bidden, Eros then produced three golden apples from his bag. He passed these on to his mother and she in turn passed them to Hippomenes. As you run and you see that she is just in front of you, you must roll one of these golden apples across her path. She will be curious, and she will stop to collect it. This will slow her down enough for you to pass her and for you to take the lead. You have three apples so you will have three chances to overtake her. Use them wisely or sadly, you too will die.' Aphrodite and Eros left his tent and returned to the crowd to watch the race.

Hippomenes walked naked to the start line of the race. He had a sash containing the three golden apples about his torso. Atalanta dropped her clothing once more. She looked enquiringly at the sash.

'It is food for the race,' he explained. 'I will need to keep my energy levels up,' he explained as he smiled.

She smiled in response, but her smile quickly faded as she now believed that she truly felt an attraction for this man. She felt an overwhelming sadness that he was about to die. She did not think him a competitive runner, or an egotistical male. She was deeply troubled about his fate and hoped her competitive spirit would allow him to win the race.

The race began and for a while they were able to keep pace with each other. As Atalanta ran she knew she was truly conflicted. She wanted and needed her freedom, but she also wanted this wonderful man to live. To her, running was as natural as breathing, so slowly she pulled slightly ahead of him, willing him to speed up. It was at this point that Hippomenes pulled out the first apple and threw it diagonally past her and it rolled slightly off to the left of the path. She was immediately distracted by the golden apple and so Atalanta slowed to gather up the apple. Amazed by its beauty she stopped and examined it, and she immediately became totally captivated by its golden lustre. She suddenly realised that Hippomenes had passed her and well in front, so she immediately gave chase. She could see that Hippomenes was tiring and soon, she was in the lead once more. He reached into his sash, and he rolled the second apple across her path. She wanted that one also but knowing what it was she took much less time to retrieve it and no time to examine it. His lead was only brief this time. As they neared the finish line, Hippomenes could see the crowds and the executioners. They cheered him on realising his strategy. They were now willing him to win. He threw the final apple and as she slowed down to pick it up, she seemingly stumbled. He passed her once more and crossed the finish line in front of her, winning the race. The crowd roared their approval and even the executioners were pleased for him and cheered swords waving high in the air.

The lovers were so full of their own happiness, that they inadvertently forgot to pay true tribute to Aphrodite. Aphrodite was now enraged, and she became incensed at their ingratitude. So, after their wedding ceremony, and whilst they busy consummating their newfound happiness with lovemaking, she caused them both to be changed permanently into a lion and a lioness.

Aphrodite proved once more that she was a goddess that took unkindly to any offence.

***

There were many events that occurred leading up to the actual start of the war between the Greeks and the Trojans. It was a war that was never formally declared. The Greeks wanted the safe return of Helen, and they were prepared to do everything possible to get her back. Ironically, the events that reportedly occurred can all be traced back to when Thetis first accepted Peleus's proposal of marriage, which was many years before Paris and Helen fled to Troy.

Thetis had met Peleus and during their brief time together they fell deeply in love in the days before the departure of the Argo. Peleus was an Argonaut, and he was a part of Jason's crew who were committed to the recovery of the Golden Fleece. Peleus was a mortal man and Thetis was an immortal sea nymph. They fell totally in love when she came to inspect the Argo's seaworthiness in the days leading up to their departure. Whilst sad by their imminent separation, and desperate to commit to each other, they made a promise to marry as soon as he returned home to her.

Peleus and the Argo were gone for a long time, but his love for her never diminished. Thetis was also true to her word and waited patiently for the two of them to be reunited and for them to be bound forever in loving matrimony.

Because it was unusual for an immortal nymph to marry a mortal man, everyone who was anyone wanted to be at their wedding. Apart from witnessing their union and celebrating their commitment to each other it promised to be the party to be seen at. Even by Mount Olympus standards, this wedding was a big event. Everything was thought of and planned to the smallest detail. It was well catered for and well attended. However, for some unknown reason, Eris, the goddess of strife and discord, did not get her invitation. This may have been a clerical error, but given Eris's reputation for violence and trouble making, it may also have been an oversight by design. Either way, Eris was both disappointed and angry, as everyone else from Ares's palace was going. It seemed that she was the only one without an invitation. Ares even offered to arrange an invitation for her.

She could be his plus one, but Eris would not hear of it. She was not invited, and so she was not going. She also became increasingly bitter about it. To stir up trouble, she crafted an ornate golden apple on which she inscribed the words, "for the fairest." She then publicly challenged the goddesses to "prove their worthiness," to claim the title and the trophy.

Now, this seemingly bit of minor mischievousness had dire, and sadly long-lasting consequences. Naturally, nearly all the goddesses claimed to be the fairest, but in the end, it became a bitter battle of wits between Aphrodite, Hera, and Athena as to who would redeem the prize. The three started fighting over an ornamental apple and it was hampering the wedding preparations, and furthermore, it threatened the overall happiness of all who resided at Mount Olympus.

It was Zeus who had decided that he had the solution to their problem. He knew a Trojan prince named Paris who had a reputation for being fair and reasonable. He would be an impartial judge who would decide which of the women deserved the golden apple. Zeus arranged with Hermes to escort the three women to the famed walled city of Troy, but only after they each agreed that they would benignly and graciously accept Paris's ruling.

Paris met with the women in a civic ceremony welcoming them to Troy. After meeting with each of them he immediately regretted accepting what he determined was an impossible task. Whatever he decided, he would be burdened with the considerable wrath of at least two out of these three exceptionally powerful goddesses. All three women had fierce reputations, and he knew that they didn't like losing Now they were at Paris's mercy, and he knew that by announcing his determination that he has at some personal risk, despite Zeus's reassurances.

So, each woman now contrived on how to best to induce Paris into choosing them. In a secret rendezvous, Hera offered Paris dominion over the whole world of mortal men. But this did not appeal to Paris at all as he had enough challenges just being a Prince of Troy. He told her that he did not want the additional aggravation. He then reprimanded her for trying to influence him, as Hera in her indignation, looked like she was planning to do him some harm.

Later, in a separate private meeting, Athena offered him her assurance that by choosing her, he would win every battle in which he fought. But this bribe also failed to entice Paris as he was a peace-loving man and only wanted a harmonious prosperity for all his people. He believed that both the human loss of life, and financial cost of battles, was always high. He told her that he wanted no part of it. He then admonished her for trying to sway his decision in this way. Athena was at once apologetic and expressed her sincere regret for doing so.

Lastly, Aphrodite approached him discreetly and she offered him the unconditional love of a most beautiful woman of Sparta named Helen. Helen was famed for being the daughter of a former King of Sparta, and for being the sister of the famous Greek hero's, Castor and Polydeuces. Aphrodite had learned of his secret desire for Helen through her palace informants, and she believed she could use his fondness for her to win her the coveted prize.

Helen was not only stunningly beautiful, but she had strikingly long blond hair and dazzling blue eyes, and both were a rarity among Greek women. It was true that she was already married, but it was widely known that she was not happy with her husband and had plans to leave him. Paris readily accepted Aphrodite's offer, as he'd always desired Helen, and had deeply regretted missing out on having her as his own bride during a earlier brief period of courtship. Helen had turned him down when she decided to marry Menelaus, the King of Sparta. She had only chosen her sister Clytemnestra's brother-in law, because she knew him to be kind and fair, and at the time, she didn't really know, or trust any of her other suitors. For her, he seemed a safe option. But even after having several children with him, she didn't feel that she truly loved him.

So, Paris agreed to Aphrodite's offer and awarded her the Golden Apple. She immediately took it upon herself to announce to everyone that she was judged to be the fairest. She strutted about, lauding the prize in front of the others. Hera and Athena immediately downplayed their loss and all the others quickly lost interest.

Paris however, immediately set about making plans to visit Sparta. In the guise of improving trading relationships between them, he and his entourage set sail. Soon he could woo Helen and he hoped that she would agree to flee with him to Troy. When Paris arrived at Menelaus's palace, he was confident that he'd be leaving it with Helen. Paris and his team were warmly welcomed by the king and the two famous brothers of Helen, Castor and Polydeuces, who were at the palace visiting their sister. They discussed beneficial trade deals, and then they arranged a feast for Paris and his retinue to celebrate his regal presence in a kingly fashion. Paris and his men only pretended to drink the wine, and they were pleased that their hosts were soon heavily under Dionysus's influence. He kept an eye on Helen and he was pleased that she too had chosen to remain sober. She had discreetly aimed many smiles and looks of admiration and interest toward him, and he now felt positive about winning her over. When he spied Helen leaving the feasting hall, he took the opportunity to follow her. As he did so, he indicated to his men that they should now leave and head for the ships to make them ready for an immediate departure.

He was pleasantly relieved when he discovered that she was eagerly waiting for him. She threw herself into his arms and declared her unconditional love for him. She begged his forgiveness for not choosing him to begin with, a decision that she had always regretted. Paris was ecstatic when he realised that Aphrodite had fulfilled her promise.

'I have already packed, and I am ready to leave with you,' Helen told a pleasantly surprised but very happy Paris.

They rushed to her rooms and where he discovered that her loyal servants had already packed her clothing, gold, jewellery, and her other valuable possessions, and they were now waiting for departure instructions. Paris did not hesitate; he was well aware of the danger. Whilst his hosts slept, Paris, Helen, and her staff deserted the palace, and they quietly made the journey down to the ships. Soon, they set sail and were well on their way to Troy.

The following morning, when the palace stirred, Menelaus awoke to discover that his wife was missing. His men searched the palace and the environs, but they could not find her. But they had discovered that all of her clothing and a great fortune in gold and jewellery were also missing. Menelaus loved his wife and believed that she truly loved him in return. His immediate conclusion was that she was kidnapped, abducted against her will, in a raid that was meticulously planned by Paris to steal his wife and his fortune. Menelaus was outraged. He summoned messengers to be sent to his brother Agamemnon, King of Mycenae and to the other kings that he had befriended .

Soon Menelaus had amassed a massive army and a huge fleet of warships. He was committed to rescuing his beloved Helen and destroying those thieving Trojans. The other kings had agreed to side with him on the proviso that Mycenae's brother, Agamemnon would take charge to lead them. Agamemnon was formidable and his experience and reputation greatly exceeded that of Menelaus, so he reluctantly agreed to Agamemnon's leadership.

The resultant war with Troy lasted over ten years. Reputedly, the warships made over one thousand one hundred crossings to transport the over 100,000 Greek warriors, their weapons, and supplies, which fought the Trojans over the ten-year campaign. There were many gods and goddesses who joined one side or the other. Aphrodite was naturally on Paris's side. Perhaps she felt some guilt in provoking the war in the first place. She had also convinced Ares and his team to side with the Trojan's. Ares really did not mind which side he was on, as long as there was plenty of fighting.

Both Hera and Athena were offended by Paris's rejection, and so they sided with the Greeks, as did Poseidon, Hermes, and Hephaestus. Heph helped the Greeks by modernising their weapons and shields. Achilles, the son of Thetis and Peleus who was actually conceived during a brief coitus just prior to the departure of the Argo, featured prominently as a legendary warrior fighting for the Greeks.

Ares eventually switched sides, but that may have been in some part due to his mother's insistence.

Only Zeus, Hades, Demeter, and Hestia remained impartial. The true reason why Zeus remained neutral was never revealed. Zeus was credited with being the father of Troy and he may have been conflicted about which side to fight for. This was clearly a civil war to him. It could also have been that as Zeus had fathered Helen with Helen's mortal mother Leda, that he felt his involvement might engender further conflict between him and Hera. Or perhaps it was because he had championed Paris's ability to solve the problem with the golden apple, and that Paris had ultimately let them down by taking Helen, that he decided to stay away from the conflict.

The war was protracted with numerous bloody, and yet unreported atrocities. At its onset, Paris pleaded with the Greeks to avert the war. He quickly offered to return all the gold and jewellery that Helen had brought with her, and he even offered more as compensation. But he could not bear to part with Helen and besides, Helen vowed that she would never leave him. The war concluded when the Trojans mistakenly accepted a giant wheeled wooden horse figurine as a symbol of peace. They unthinkingly brought the wooden horse into the city walls through their impregnable gates in the mistaken belief that it was a symbol of the Greeks desire for peace. Helen had begged the military commanders not to do so, fearing a Greek trick, but they ignored her, and so now the Greeks subterfuge was in motion. In the darkness of the night, the secreted Greek warriors, led by Odysseus, exited the wooden horse, and opened the fortress doors to give entry to the Greek army. They quickly took control of the city, tortured, and enslaved its peoples, and plundered their wealth. Paris died during the war but Helen somehow survived. When he confronted her, Menelaus saw her grief and mistakenly believed that it was for her regret in leaving him. He forgave Helen for her unfaithfulness and now just wanted to take her home.

Troy, and its citizens, never recovered. Some of the survivors made their way by sailing ships to Italy to start a new life.

We do not know how Aphrodite reacted to the brutal war between the Greeks and the Trojans. It was believed that she never intended for it to happen and was for the most part unaware of the worst aspects of the brutality. The wedding, the dispute over the apple, and Aphrodite's manipulation of Paris, may have inadvertently caused the war, but she was nowhere to be seen at the conclusion.

***

The Goddess Aphrodite did not have a traditional list of tasks, chores, or any serious responsibilities at Mount Olympus. She saw her contribution to mortals simply to be worshipped as their goddess of beauty, desire, lust, romance, and a symbol of the promise of great sex. She sometimes got bored with all their adoration, and occasionally she desired a change of scenery. When Ares told her of his plans to travel to Mesopotamia to discuss a forthcoming battle with their king, she decided to surprise him by meeting him there for what would appear to be an impromptu passionate rendezvous. It would be such fun. Eros decided to accompany his mother, and so Eros bid his farewell to Psyche with an assurance that he would be home soon.

It was at the same time that Typhon had decided to make one last attempt in seducing his beloved Aphrodite. Unfortunately for him, he arrived at Mount Olympus just days after Aphrodite and Eros had departed. A helpful stranger was able to point out the direction the goddess and her son had taken, but he was unaware of their destination. Typhon gratefully thanked the man and set off in excited pursuit. Typhon could fly fast, and he made no attempt to hide himself as he scoured the countryside looking for Aphrodite. He figured that with Aphrodite being away from Mount Olympus, she would not have the protection of Zeus, or Ares, or her clever former husband, Hephaestus. This would be his best opportunity to demonstrate his love and devotion to her. He hoped he would somehow fully win her love.

Ares was accompanied by Athena. She liked to be there to moderate the discussions between warring leaders, and to dampen Ares's enthusiasm for his use of brute force aggression. If she could work in a peaceful solution into the discussions, she would present it. If that did not work, then she would offer her plans for a victory that would cause the least amount of bloodshed and suffering. Ares tolerated Athena's participation, as she was wise and respected, and also because she was most often right. Athena never contradicted him or chastised him and for this he respected her even more. Ares figured that she helped make him look good. As a war god, Ares readily understood that image and reputation was everything.

Once the war plans were set, Athena stayed to instruct the king and his officers in the details and the scope of their campaign. She offered helpful advice on logistics and reinforcements. She checked their weapons, provisions, horses, and carriages. She was a real detail person. While she was busy, Ares returned home to Mount Olympus to fetch his weapons and his team.

When Aphrodite and Eros entered the military camp, the guards immediately recognised them. As a delightful discussion about non-military topics, they decided in Ares's absence to escorted them to Athena.

When they entered the tent, they were surprised to see Athena and not Ares. 'Athena? What are you doing here?' Aphrodite was puzzled to see the goddess at the military camp where she had planned her surprise sexual tryst with Ares.

'Aphrodite. Eros. Why are you here?' Athena was equally surprised. 'You do know that this will soon become a war zone.'

'I've come to surprise, Ares. Eros is only here as my protector,' she explained and smiled as she gave her son a one-armed playful hug.

'I am sorry to tell you, but the surprise is on you. Ares has returned to Mount Olympus,' Athena explained.

'What!' Aphrodite was angry. She hated it when her plans didn't work out her way. 'When will he be back? Is this battle happening, or what?' she demanded.

'Sadly, the battle is happening. The fighting men are ready, and we now await Ares's return with Deimos, Phobos, Eris, and Enyo. They are bringing such weapons that will make it a swift victory.'

'We will wait for him,' Aphrodite decided. She started looking about her for a place to rest. The area was dry and dusty, and she was tired from their journey. 'Where is Ares's tent?'

'I'll take you to it,' Athena offered.

'Aphrodite!' a voice called.

The three turned to see a tall, ugly man enter the tent and stride purposefully toward them.

'It's Typhon!' Athena announced as she drew her sword and grabbed her shield ready to fight and protect Aphrodite. Eros had already nocked an arrow in his bow and was ready to let it fly.

'No, wait!' Typhon cried holding his arms up in capitulation. 'Can you not see that I come to you in peace and love,' he declared.

'Peace and love?' Aphrodite was confused.

Typhon came nearer, undaunted by the sword and arrow pointed directly at his body. He bent on one knee and with his hand on his heart, he spoke sincerely. 'Aphrodite. I am your greatest admirer and I love you the most. Be with me and I will love, protect, and serve you like no other man ever could or would.'

'No,' she replied.

'No?' Typhon was confused. This strategy had worked perfectly in his mind.

'No,' she repeated.

'Why?' he demanded.

'Because you are ugly, smelly, and you are a monster,' she explained as a matter of fact.

'I can change,' he offered.

'Never,' Aphrodite made it decisively clear that she did not want him.

Typhon blushed crimson. His body swelled and his neck bulged. Soon extra arms and hands emerged from his torso and then numerous snake and dragon heads sprouted from his head.

Eros let fly numerous arrows in rapid succession, but they bounced ineffectually off Typhon's skin.

As Typhon was about to launch deadly poison, Athena yelled her command to the two others. 'Run!'

The three started running for their lives. They ran toward a rocky outcrop well away from the camp. Presently a spiralling wind chased them, flattening the tents within the encampment, scattering men, weapons, and horses. The dust and sand flew in all directions and mercilessly pelted Aphrodite, Eros, and Athena.

They ran and ran, and soon the mighty Euphrates River was in front of them blocking their escape. Athena hesitated, and then turned back to seek protection from a clump of boulders.

'We'll jump into the river!' Aphrodite yelled her order to Eros above the din of the wind and sand.

'I cannot swim!' Eros yelled back. 'I am scared that I will drown,' he said, and he was clearly frightened.

Aphrodite loudly detailed her plan for their survival. 'I will turn us into fish so that we can breathe underwater. There, we will wait for the sandstorm to pass over us, and for Typhon to give up and go away.'

As they jumped into the deep water, Aphrodite changed them both into fish. They swam deep and mingled with the other fish and soon they felt safe, and they began to relax. They had escaped from Typhon's fury.

Athena however, had covered herself with her shield and cloak. In this way she was protected from the billowing sands that quickly covered her prone form.

Aphrodite and Eros were hungry, and so they followed the other fish's example and began to graze on the abundant food on the rivers bed. They were safe, happy, and comfortable, and soon they forgot that they were once Aphrodite and Eros, a Goddess and God from Mount Olympus. They happily stayed in the river, and they forever remained as fish.

Eventually, Typhon gave up his windstorm. He could not find Aphrodite and he eventually resolved to himself that Aphrodite would never be his. And so, he returned to home to Echidna, and he remained with her for the rest of his life.

When the sandstorm stopped, Athena shed her cloak and shield and began to look for Aphrodite and Eros. She had overheard Aphrodite's plan to change them into fish, so that they could survive underwater. She sat by the riverbank for several days, but neither Aphrodite nor Eros came to her. Saddened by their fate, Athena held up her hands and cast their images as the two fishes into the night sky, which came to be known to us, as the constellation "Pisces".

***

In Roman times, the mythology of Aphrodite was renamed by the Romans as the Goddess Venus. She had all the same attributes as the Greek Aphrodite, but the Roman's preferred to rename most of the Gods they adopted from other cultures.

***

Book one - Pisces

The Greek Constellations series of books.

The ancient Greeks identified and named Forty-Eight out of the Eighty-Eight recognised constellations. They were catalogued by a Greek astronomer Claudius Ptolemy in his publication the Almagest around 150 CE. The origins of the mythological stories that identified the constellations predate this documentation by as much as a thousand years.

Book one - the constellation Pisces and a modern retelling of the story of Aphrodite and Eros and how they became the "Two Fish".

Aphrodite is well known as the Greek goddess of love, romance, and sexuality. Aphrodite is also known to us as Venus, and the planet is named after her in her honour. This is the story of how Aphrodite came to be. Born in the ocean during a struggle between father and son, she was raised on an island. As an adult she was carried by Zeus to Mount Olympus to work and play with the gods and goddesses who resided there.

After a brief marriage to Hephaestus, she formed a steamy relationship with Hephaestus's brother, Ares and together they had a son they named Eros. All her life, she struggled with the unwanted, yet amorous advances of a Titan monster named, Typhon. Eventually, she and Eros had to flee Mount Olympus to escape his wrath, and they became the constellation of the two fish, known to us as *Pisces*.

This book is also available as an E-Book

Book two – Capricorn

The constellation of Capricorn and the story of Pricus the Sea-Goat.

Pricus is an old sea-goat with a problem. He is regarded as the old man of the sea. The younger generation wants desperately to abandon the old ways and leave their ocean home to live a more adventurous life on the land. The sea-goats were able to morph from sea-goats into land goats when they emerge from the surf to walk on land. They quickly learn to morph into human form, and to their delight discover that they can have much more fun exploring the plethora of opportunities that await them. In their naivety they make many mistakes, some ending in tragedy. Pricus is desperate to save the younger generation from themselves, and so must become increasingly resourceful do so, and do so in such a way that his solution remains permanent. His dedication to his own kind earns him his place as the constellation of the sea-goat, known to us as Capricornus or Capricorn.

Planned launch 2027

Book three - Pandora (Saturn's moon)

Pandora. A modern retelling of the story of how she came to be the first woman.

Zeus, king of the Greek God's, commissioned his son Hephaestus to craft the a human woman who would become the role model for all human woman. Aided by Athena, Hephaestus carefully researched the perfect form, and then moulded her from clay. He then skillfully painted her and glazed her into his image of the perfect woman. After being fired in his kiln, she was given the breath of life by the wind god Zephyr. She was named Pandora, being the bearer of the gifts bequeathed to her by the gods and goddesses of Mount Olympus. Zeus then commanded that she be properly trained so that she could confidently navigate life's complexities, but her tutors went too far with her, and she becomes too powerful to live as a normal human. Zeus became disillusioned with her, and so he decided that she should be married off to a minor god, so that she would do no harm to herself, or to others.

Pandora's story is a great example of how easy it is to be led a stray by undesirable role models. Her story is so significant that she is also honoured as Pandora, one of Saturn's moons.

This book is now also available as an E-Book

Book four - Taurus

The constellation Taurus and modern retelling of the story of Europa and her meeting with Zeus as the white bull.

When Zeus, king and master of the gods and goddesses of Mount Olympus finds himself between wives he sets out on a desperate search for the perfect woman to marry. On a sunny field, set among spring flowers, on a stretch of land next to the sea, he finds her. She is Europa, a gorgeous African princess. For Zeus, it becomes love at first sight. In his infatuation for this woman, he tries numerous times to impress her, and almost succeeds. Sadly, for Zeus, his one true love is betrothed to another, and sadly for Zeus, a daughter must do her duty. Disguised as a magnificent white bull, he tries one last desperate attempt to have her. The consequences of his quest for true love are celebrated as the constellation of the white bull, know to us as the Taurus.

Also included in this story is the Constellation Draco, known as Ladon the Dragon and Laelaps as the Constellation Canis Major or Greater Dog, and the Teumessian Fox as the Constellation Canis Minor or Lesser Dog.

This book is now also available as an E-Book

Book five - Scorpio and Orion

The constellations Scorpio and Orion and the story of the scorpion verse the hunter.

Artemis is the goddess of the forests and of the hunt. She befriends a hunter named Orion. Their friendship is slowly progressing toward a blossoming romance when Orion boasts of his ability to wantonly kill all the animals that cross his path. Artemis is dismayed. Her policy is to only kill for food, to kill for pleasure is an outrage. She feels she must sacrifice her future relationship by stopping Orion from completing his boast. She manifests a giant scorpion and sends it to attack and destroy Orion. A massive battle ensues and both are defeated, thus preserving animal life from indiscriminate killings. To celebrate the outcome and to remind us that all life is precious, their images are cast into the heavens as the constellation *Orion* and the constellation of the Scorpion known to us as *Scorpio*.

Planned launch 2026

Book six - Aries

The constellation Aries and a modern retelling of the story of Chrysomallos the Ram and Princess Helle.

Born from a union between Poseidon and Theophane on a remote island that was the home of a flock of sheep. They are interrupted by shepherds during copulation, so they disguised themselves as sheep to avoid the embarrassment that Theophane might suffer if their tryst became public knowledge. Their male child is born with the ability to morph from human form into a ram. From his father, he has long golden hair, and when he becomes a ram, he has golden fleece. He has wings and the ability to fly.

He is named Chrysomallos and he is raised by his loving mother Theophane. He eventually befriends princess Helle who lives in a nearby kingdom. When their lives became perilous, Chrysomallos the flying, golden fleeced Ram, comes to their rescue. His bravery is celebrated as the constellation of the Ram, know to us as *Aries*.

This book is also available as an E-Book.

Book seven - Ophiuchus

The constellation of Ophiuchus and the story of Asclepius the serpentius or serpent bearer.

Asclepius was the son of Apollo. When Apollo had to rescue Asclepius from his dying mother's womb, he realised that he did not know enough about medicine and surgery, and so he set about discovering as much as he could. He later taught all that he learned to his son. Next, to further his education, Apollo decided that Asclepius would learn even more from the tutor Chiron. Through him he completed his training and went on to be the foremost authority on how to manage illness and repair injuries. His wife Epione and he had five daughters and three sons, and all became involved in the practice of medical treatments. The most prominent daughter was Hygieia and the practice of hygiene is named after her.

Both Apollo and Asclepius have been forever revered as the fathers of medical treatments and their names were included in the original Hippocratic Oath, that all medical practitioners swore upon when becoming formally registered to become doctors.

His dedication to healing the sick and injured was commemorated in the night sky as the constellation *Ophiuchus*. Many people who practice in astrology believe that Ophiuchus is the unrecognised thirteenth star sign.

Also featured is the constellation of *Serpens* or "The Snake," who Asclepius witnessed bringing healing herbs to another snake who was sick, and this event started him on his discovery of benefits of medicinal herbs.

Planned launch 2028

Book eight - Cancer and Leo

The constellations of Cancer & Leo, and a modern retelling of the stories of Karkinos the giant crab, Zosma the Nemean lioness, Astron the hydra, Aquila the eagle, Sagitta the arrow, and the constellation named after Herakles the Demi-God.

The birth of Herakles was surrounded by controversy. Being the demi-god son of the King of all the gods, he found it difficult to live a routine life with his wife and children.

Herakles was persecuted by Hera for being her husband Zeus's illegitimate son, and so he was inflicted by incessant painful headaches. He was told of a remedy by the oracle in Delphi, but before he could be cured, it required him to agree to take on many incredible tasks which were assigned to him by the local king. By completing these labours, he would be able to go on and live a long and fulfilling life.

He later became immortal, and Herakles is forever remembered as a Greek Mythological hero for defeating the giant crab that became known as constellation Cancer. He also killed the man-eating lioness that became known as the constellation Leo. He slew the serpent of Lake Lerna, which is now known as the constellation Hydra.

Herakles used his arrow which now known as the constellation Sagitta to kill a giant eagle that became to be known as the constellation Aquila or "The Eagle".

Herakles was finally accepted at Mount Olympus and was honoured with the constellation Herakles also known by many as Hercules.

This book is also available in E-Book format.

Book nine - Gemini

The constellation Gemini and a modern retelling of the story of the twins, Castor and Polydeuces.

Leucippe was desperate to become a grandmother. Fed up with her son-in-law's lack of progress, she asked Zeus for help. When Zeus arrived, he took the opportunity, disguised himself as a swan, and then he did much more than just arrange for Leda to become pregnant.

The Spartan twins grew up to become skilled horsemen, hunters, warriors, and adventurers. They embarked on many journeys together and their adventures included sailing on the Argo with Jason on his quest for the golden fleece, being hunters at the Calydonian wild boar hunt, and fighting Trojans at Troy. It was their sister Helen who was the central reason for that protracted war.

The twins were honoured by Zeus for their bravery and commitment to each other, and he cast their image into the night sky to be forever remembered as the constellation of the Twins, which is now known as *Gemini*. Also featured in this story is the constellation The Swan or *Cygnus*.

This book is also available as an E-Book.

Book ten - Virgo and Libra

The constellations of Virgo & Libra and modern retelling the story of the Astraea the maiden, and Themis the scales.

Astraea and Themis were both goddesses who were committed to advancing the living conditions of the humans who lived on the island of Thera. Along with other gods and goddess they believed that they would become the role models for all future human progress advancements.

Astraea strongly believed in justice and sort punishment for those that transgressed against the common good. Her belief was that punishment was a deterrent and that the formal process of trial and conviction for those found guilty of a crime had a place in society.

Themis was more about bringing about restitution to an aggrieved person who was treated unfairly by another. Her mediation skills gave rise to the belief that there was always a remedy when agreements fell apart.

However, the speed of their progress and their intentions to achieve self-determination worried Zeus. After inspecting the work and assessing all that had been achieved, he concluded that it must end abruptly. And as every Greek immortal knows, when Zeus is determined and has made up his mind, nothing stops his decision from happening.

For Astraea, the decision was devastating and so she cast herself into the night sky as "the maiden", forever watching over humanity as the constellation *Virgo*.

Themis was later honoured for her balanced outlook on life and is remembered as the scales as she evenly balanced out her reasoning and decisions. She is now known to us as the constellation **Libra**.

This book is also available in E-Book format.

Book eleven – Aquarius

The constellation Aquarius and a modern retelling of the story of Ganymede the water-bearer.

Ganymede was adopted by a family of shepherds when he was found abandoned as a young child. He preferred his own company, and whilst good at caring for the sheep he was eventually regarded as a misfit by his adopted family.

One day, as he is tending the sheep, he was sighted by Zeus, who was flying past in his eagle form. Out of curiosity Zeus landed to meet the young man and became quickly became enamoured with him. Ganymede found himself attracted to the powerful God and very much wanted to be with him. Zeus easily convinced the young man to give up his shepherding life and come with him to Mount Olympus.

Ganymede became Zeus's friend and lover. He took over the role of cup bearer during important civil functions from Zeus's daughter Hebe, as she had found love and married a Greek hero. Ganymede quickly became fascinated with aqueducts and fountains, and he was responsible for improving the water quality and availability of clean drinking water to Mount Olympus's inhabitants. His contribution is celebrated as the constellation of the "water-bearer" now know to us as **Aquarius**.

This book is also available in E-Book format.

Book twelve – Sagittarius

The constellation of Sagittarius and the story of the "Archer" Crotus.

A water Naiad nymph named Eupheme was a demi-goddess of the Hippocrene freshwater spring near Mount Helicon. She was youthful, very beautiful, and powerful. She met and had a relationship with the God Pan, a Satyr, famous for playing the pipes was the god of shepherds, flocks, rustic musicians, and improvisation. Their romance led to the birth of Crotus.

Crotus was a Satyr and grew up to be like his like his father, preferring the company of muses. Most Satyrs preferred the company of Dionysus, God of wine, revelry, and debauchery, so Crotus was unusual in this way.

The muses were providers of inspiration to artists, musicians, poets, story tellers, artisans, entertainers, and dancers. They brought out the natural talents of those they inspired, and positively encouraged them to excel by pursuing their passions and striving for perfection in their chosen art form.

Crotus was also a great hunter and many say that he invented the hunting bow. He was more popular as a musician and his most noteworthy contribution to performance music was the addition of rhythmic beats used to accompany the musician's musical score. He was also responsible for the introduction of a ritual applause to signify both pleasure from the performance and gratitude to the artist for their dedication to the composition and the quality of the performance. The applause was widely recognised as a significant motivator for artistic excellence.

Crotus was a mortal, and when he died, the Younger Muses petitioned Zeus to have his likeness immortalised as place in the night sky. Their petition was positively received and, in his honour, he created the constellation of the Archer which is known to us as **Sagittarius**.

Planned launch 2028

Book thirteen – Centaurus

The constellation Centaurus and the story of the tutor Cheiron.

Cheiron was a centaur who became the tutor to many of the legendary heroes of Greek mythology. Unlike other centaurs, Cheiron was intelligent, civilised and very kind. He was the teacher of students that included Jason, Castor, Polydeuces, Asclepius, Peleus, and Achilles and he taught them philosophy, archery, hunting, medicine, music, gymnastics, and the art of prophecy.

His life ended tragically when he was accidently struck with a poisoned arrow by his close friend, Herakles. Herakles had loosed the arrow in an attempt to ward off marauding cruel centaurs who came to cause mischief to Cheiron, but in the confusion, Cheiron stepped into the path of the arrow and was stuck. His immortality prevented his death, but the strong   poison caused him everlasting agony. He decided to surrender his immortality to Zeus so that he could pass into the underworld. He was then commemorated as the constellation of the Centaur and is known to us as **Centaurus.**

Planned launch 2028

The other Greek constellations that are yet to be featured include Andromeda, Ara, Auriga, Boötes, Cassiopeia, Cepheus, Corona Australis, Corona Borealis, Corvus, Crater, Delphinus, Equuleus, Eridanus, Lepus, Lupus, Lyra, Pegasus, Perseus, Piscis Austrinus, Triangulum, Ursa Major, Ursa Minor, and Argo Navis (now divided into Carina, Puppis, and Vela)

Follicle Farm – A novel adventure. (Fiction)

Follicle Farm – A novel adventure. (Fiction)

Follicle Farm is a comical and imaginative insight into organisational structure and behaviour of the trillions of cells that make up the microscopic world of every living person. It reveals how cells within the human body really think and how they, mostly, work well together. Bobby is a Mitochondria, and he works as a humble Follicle Farmer. He, with millions of colleagues, are part of the amazing organisation dedicated to growing hair for the human male that they live inside of. Recently, Bobby made an important discovery when he learned how to reverse the effects of alopecia and greying hair. Now it's up to management to debate if they should use his technique.

Join Bobby as he travels the body, ably assisted by Banjo and Skip, as he meets and deals with other human cells in various systems throughout the body. Bobby quickly learns there is more to management than just servicing the body's needs. Cliques, quirks, politics, unions, and hidden agendas, all thrive in Bobby's world.

You'll share in his adventure of personal growth as he encourages other Follicle Farmers to utilises best practices in growing quality hair.

This book is now available in Paperback or E-Book

Your concise guide to the meaning of life.

Your concise guide to the meaning of life. (Non-Fiction)

This is a serious book designed to help people. Its main purpose is to assist you on how to gain insights on how to live a happier and more fulfilled life. It will give the you, the reader, instant benefits. It is peppered with many great quotes, many of them are my own. I've combined my interest in philosophy, sociology, psychology, and history to delve into the true meaning of life. The reader will not only understand why they are here, but how to make their experience more meaningful.

My main aim is to inspire readers into taking more control of how they make decisions that positively affect their achievements, successes, happiness, and therefore their well-being. The book is a summary of concise points that are easy to learn and apply to the readers life for an immediate benefit. It includes popular relevant quotes to re-enforce the messages and teaching. I have also included personal anecdotes that give real life and meaningful examples of how the material applies to all readers.

Topics include

- an explanation the main purpose for living.
- how to improve your relationships.
- how communication works and how to make it more effective.
- understanding your needs and desires and how to improve outcomes for yourself.
- understanding what motivates other people.

- how to exceed your own expectations.
- understanding your own personal legal, moral, ethical, and value system.
- improving your control over your emotions.
- understanding the concepts of faith, fate and fairness.
- and being better prepared for the final stages of your life.

This book is now available in Paperback or E-Book